CRUSADE OF EAGLES

WILLIAM W. JOHNSTONE
WITH J. A. JOHNSTONE

WHEELER PUBLISHING
A part of Gale, Cengage Learning

GALE
CENGAGE Learning·

Detroit • New York • San Francisco • New Haven, Conn • Waterville, Maine • London

GALE
CENGAGE Learning®

LIBRARY OF CONGRESS CATALOGING-IN-PUBLICATION DATA

Johnstone, William W.
   Crusade of eagles / by William W. Johnstone with J.A. Johnstone. — Large print ed.
      p. cm. — (Wheeler Publishing large print western)
   ISBN-13: 978-1-4104-4566-7 (pbk.)
   ISBN-10: 1-4104-4566-6 (pbk.)
   1. Large type books. 2. Kidnapping—Fiction. 3. Frontier and pioneer life—Fiction. 4. Domestic fiction. I. Johnstone, J. A. II. Title.
PS3560.O415C78 2012
813'.54—dc23   2012001785

Published in 2012 by arrangement with Pinnacle Books, an imprint of Kensington Publishing Corp.

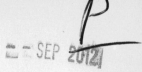
CRUSADE OF EAGLES

CRUSADE OF EAGLES

CHAPTER ONE

The cold rain had begun before dawn, and continued to slash down on the small relay station that was the last stop before Colorado Springs. Looming blackly in the night was a large green Concord stage with yellow letters proudly proclaiming the carrier: MACCALLISTER STAGE LINES. It had rolled into the station at nine o'clock the night before, drawn by eight prancing horses blowing fog in the cold night air, and driven by a wizened old driver who pulled the team to a halt.

There had been six passengers on board the stage, four men, one woman, and her nine-year-old daughter, and they had stepped down from the stage exhausted and grateful for the sparse comfort offered by the way station for the night. Their luggage had remained in the tightly lashed leather boot, dry and secure despite the rain that had started this morning. The window curtain, however, did little to keep out the rain, and the hard leather seats would be cold and wet for today's travel.

Last night, the six had eaten a late supper of stew and biscuits provided by Gulley Andrews, the manager of the way station. After that, they went to bed, warm and dry.

Now, in the predawn darkness, Loomis Tate was sitting on a bale of hay eating cold beans from a can and looking through the rain toward the way station, which was some thirty yards distant. Loomis was a man of medium height and size, distinguished only by his pockmarked face and a drooping left eye.

Matt Logan had climbed up into the loft a little earlier and was looking toward the east. Logan was tall and thin, almost cadaverous-looking. He had an oversized nose. Ron Michaels and Ken Strayhorn were keeping warm in one of the stalls. Michaels was an albino, and even the men who rode with him found him creepy. Strayhorn was short and stocky, with red hair and a bushy beard. Drew Tate was standing in the doorway relieving himself, no more than six feet away. Although Drew was Loomis's brother, the two men didn't look anything alike. Drew was almost nice-

8

looking, until one looked into his eyes. They were obsidian, almost serpentine. He had a mustache that he groomed daily.

"What the hell, Drew, you got no more manners than to piss that close to where a man is eatin'?" Loomis growled.

"Sorry," Drew said. "Wasn't thinkin'."

"That don't surprise me none. You don't never think."

"It ain't right, you talkin' to me like that," Drew said. "We're brothers."

"The only reason we're brothers is 'cause Ma wouldn't let me'n Kelly hold your head underwater when you was born," Loomis growled.

"Yeah, well, still, you got no right to talk to me like that. Kelly don't never talk to me like that."

"Yeah, well, Kelly ain't got much more sense than you do," Loomis said, speaking of their other brother.

"It's gettin' light in the east," Logan called down from the loft. "I reckon they'll be comin' out soon."

"Get the horses ready," Loomis ordered. "Soon as we get the money, we'll be ridin' out of here."

"How come we don't just hold 'em up out on the road?" Drew asked. "I ain't never heard of robbin' a stagecoach afore it even leaves the station."

"No, and neither has anybody else, which is exactly why we're a'doin' it this a'way," Loomis replied. "Doin' it like this means there ain't no chance they can get away from us. And 'cause we'll catch 'em by surprise, more'n likely, they won't put up no fight."

"Lights on in the house," Logan called down. "They's folks movin' around inside."

"Won't be long now," Loomis said.

Inside the way station, the kitchen was filled with the rich aroma of coffee and frying bacon. Falcon MacCallister was in the kitchen, leaning against the sideboard, drinking coffee as he watched Gulley Andrews and his wife, Mary, preparing breakfast for the coach passengers.

"Normally, we don't 'low no passengers in here till breakfast time," Gulley said. He chuckled. "But seein' as you ain't just a passenger, but are a partner in the stage company, I reckon you're welcome."

"Well, I appreciate that, Gulley," Falcon said. "But if you want me to wait somewhere else, I'll be glad to go back to my room till you call."

"No, no. The only reason I don't like folks in here is 'cause I don't like nobody lookin' over our shoulder when we're a'cookin'. They keep trying to tell us a better way of doin' things," Gulley said as he removed a couple of pans of biscuits.

"If it was me, I'd leave the biscuits in a mite longer," Falcon said.

"What?" Gulley asked, looking up quickly. Then, seeing the smile on Falcon's face, he realized Falcon was teasing, and he laughed. "Well, if you don't like the way I make my biscuits, you don't have to eat them," he said.

"No, no!" Falcon said, holding up his hands in surrender. "I'll eat your biscuits. Mary's gravy would make anybody's biscuits taste good."

Mary laughed. "I see you know who to flatter, Mr. MacCallister," she said. She had been making gravy, and now she poured it into a big bowl.

"Uhmmm, that really looks good," Falcon said.

"Gulley, breakfast is all ready now," Mary said.

"Billy," Gulley called to the stage driver. Billy McClain and Ben Jackson, his shotgun guard, were sitting at the dining room table, drinking coffee.

"Yeah?" Billy answered.

"Call your passengers down," Gulley said.

"Breakfast is ready."

"I'll see to the team," Ben said. Ben was in his fifties, a retired army sergeant who had served all through the Civil War, as well as during several of the Indian campaigns. He had been with Reno during Custer's last fight.

"You can wait until after breakfast if you want," Billy said.

"No need. I'll just grab me a biscuit and bacon, and by the time you folks are finished eatin', why, we'll be all ready to go."

"Here you go, Ben," Mary said, cutting open a biscuit and laying on two thickly cut pieces of bacon. She handed it to the shotgun guard.

"Thanks, Mary," Ben said.

From his place in the barn, Loomis watched the back door of the house open, then slam shut as someone hurried through the dark and the rain.

"Here comes someone from the house," Loomis hissed. "Get back out of sight."

Ben slipped into the barn, then removed a match from a waxed, waterproof box to light a kerosene lantern. When the flame was turned up, a small, golden bubble of light cast long shadows inside the barn.

"Good mornin', horses. I hate to get you out of a nice warm stall on a rainy day like this, but we got a long run ahead of us," Ben said, talking to the animals. "So we may as well get started."

It was warm and dry inside the barn, though the sounds of the wind and the rain outside were testimony to the cold, wet beginning of the new day. The barn was redolent with the aromas of leather, cured wood, horseflesh, and hay. Ben walked over to the first of the eight horses that would form the hitch for the coach. He was just opening the gate to the stall when he saw someone standing in the shadows.

"Who are you?" Ben asked. "What are you doing here?"

That was as far as Ben got, because before he could say another word, a very pale hand came up from behind him and clamped down on his mouth.

"Ungghnn!" he said, trying to call out.

Another hand, equally colorless, came around, this one holding a knife. Ben felt the painful slice of the knife as it slit his throat.

One of the passengers was a whiskey drummer, going to Colorado Springs to sell his wares to the saloons there. Mac Goff was short, with a narrow face and a hooked nose. Owen Gilmore, a lawyer, was over-weight, red-faced, and sweated a lot. George Poindexter was the third male passenger, and he was young and clean-cut. The lone woman was exceptionally pretty, and her five-year-old daughter was already showing signs of being just as pretty. Falcon Mac-Callister was the fourth man.

"Darlin', I just bet you would like one of these sugar cookies I made yesterday," Mrs. Andrews said to the little girl. She looked at the girl's mother. "Is it all right to give her a cookie?"

"Yes, that's very nice of you," Mrs. Poindexter said. "What do you say, Becky?"

"Thank you," Becky said.

"Mr. MacCallister, what's a fella like you ridin' in a common stage for?" Goff asked. "Why, I'd think you'd be ridin' in your own private coach."

Falcon chuckled. "In a way, you might say I am doing that, since two of my brothers and I own this stage line."

The drummer laughed as well. "I reckon you got a point there."

"What brings you to Colorado Springs, Mr. MacCallister?" the woman asked. This was Mrs. Poindexter, and she was the wife of the dairy farmer.

"I received a letter from a man named James Pourtales," Falcon said. "He asked that I come discuss some business arrangement with him."

"Yes, that would be Count Pourtales," Mrs. Poindexter said.

"Do you know him?"

"I know him. My husband and I do business with him," Mrs. Poindexter said. "He owns a large dairy, and we sell him milk."

"I thought he owned a hotel."

The lawyer chuckled. "Ahh, that would be the Broadmoor Casino," he said. "Yes, Pourtales owns the Broadmoor. It is his attempt to bring culture to the West, I believe."

"And you think he won't be successful?"

"Have you ever heard the expression 'a silk purse from a sow's ear'?" the lawyer asked. "Any attempt to bring culture to this — godforsaken — West is akin to making a silk purse from a sow's ear."

"Well, I will withhold judgment until I've met him and seen the Broadmoor Casino," Falcon said.

"Is Ben comin' back in?" Mary asked after breakfast. "I have some biscuits and bacon left over and he likes to take a few with him."

"I'll take 'em to 'im," Billy offered. He nodded toward a shotgun, standing in the corner. "Although I'm sure he'll be back in.

That's his shotgun there, and he's not likely to leave it."

"Well, I'll just wrap his biscuit and bacon sandwiches up in a cloth," Mary said. "But you be sure and tell him not to forget."

"I'll tell him," Billy promised. He stood up, took the last swallow of his coffee, then wiped his mouth. He picked up a canvas bag with a locked top.

"All right, folks," he called to the other passengers. "If we want to make Colorado Springs by noon, we need to get under way."

Billy and the passengers started toward the door, but Falcon stopped just before he reached the door.

"I left my hat in my room," he said. "Don't leave without me."

Billy laughed. "Do you think I'd do that? It's your stage, Mr. MacCallister. I may look dumb, but I ain't dumb enough to leave my boss high and dry."

Goff laughed. "You ain't likely to leave anyone dry in this weather," he joked.

The other passengers laughed as well; then, as Falcon started back to his room, they went outside. The stage was standing where it was left the night before. There was no team attached.

"Damn," Billy said. "Ben ain't hooked up the team yet? That's not like him."

As Billy and his passengers started through the rain toward the stage, five men, with guns drawn, suddenly came from the barn.

"Hold it right there, folks," the leader of the group of men called. He had a pock-marked face and a droopy eye.

"What is this?" Billy called. "Where is Ben?"

"Ben? That'd be the fella that come out here to hitch up the team?"

"Yes."

"He's back there in the barn. Seems he sort of stuck his neck out." He giggled at his own joke.

Had an artist made a painting of the scene being played out in the yard of the way station, it would have been gray-washed by the falling rain. On one side of the canvas there was the barn and stagecoach. On the other side, the house. In between the barn and the house, Loomis and his men formed one line, while the driver and his passengers formed another line.

Becky stared pointedly at the albino.

"Mama," she said. "That man has pink eyes."

"Hush, dear!" Mrs. Poindexter said, frightened at how the albino might react.

The albino, who had endured a lifetime of

17

stares, said nothing.

"Are you the driver?" Loomis asked Billy.

"Yes. Who are you?"

"The name is Tate."

"Tate?" the lawyer said. "Would you be Loomis Tate?"

"That's me," Loomis said. He glanced toward the rotund lawyer, then nodded. "Yeah, I thought I recognized you," he said. "You're a lawyer, ain't you? I seen you back durin' one of my trials. Maybe I should have used you then. My lawyer sure didn't do me no good."

"I don't work for free," Gilmore said haughtily.

"Yeah, well, I don't know what that means," Loomis said. "But it don't matter none. The judge had his time schedule for when I was to get out of prison, and I had mine." He smiled broadly, though instead of making his face look more pleasant, it exaggerated the drooping eye and pulled the other one into a grotesque mask.

"You escaped from prison, did you?" Billy asked.

"Yeah, I did," Loomis answered. He nodded toward the bag Billy was carrying. "I take it that bag you're a'totin' over your shoulder is the money shipment bag?"

"It's an express bag," Billy said. "I don't

have no idea what's in it."

Loomis chuckled. "Well, then, that makes me smarter'n you, don't it? 'Cause I do know what's in it. You're carryin' a ten-thousand-dollar shipment to a fella by the name of James Pourtales."

"I wouldn't know about that," Billy said.

"Toss the bag over."

Billy shook his head. "I don't think I want to do that."

"What'd you say?" Loomis asked.

"I'm responsible for this shipment," Billy said. "You're goin' to have to take it from me, 'cause I ain't handin' it over."

"Michaels. You and Strayhorn bring . . ." He paused and looked at Billy. "What'd you say his name was? The man who come out for the horses?"

"Ben."

"You two drag Ben's body out here," he said. "I think the driver needs a little convincin'."

The albino and Strayhorn put their guns back in their holsters, then went into the barn. A moment later, they came back out, one holding each of Ben's legs, dragging his body through the mud behind them.

"Mama, what's wrong with him?" Becky asked.

"I killed him, little girl," the albino said.

19

"Same as I'm goin' to kill your mama if the driver doesn't do what we tell him to."

"No! Don't hurt my mama!" Becky cried, wrapping her arms around her mother's legs. Her mother pulled Becky's face into her skirt.

"Michaels, there ain't no call for you to be scarin' the little girl," Loomis said. He looked back at the driver and passengers. "But it's up to you folks whether or not she sees anyone else get kilt. You," he said, pointing to the whiskey drummer. "Take that bag off the driver's shoulder and toss it over here to us."

"Stay where you are, Goff," Falcon called down from the porch.

Loomis looked over toward the sound of the voice, and saw that another man had come from the house and was now standing out at the edge of the porch, looking down at them. His gun was still in his holster.

"What did you say, mister?" Loomis asked.

"I told Goff to stay where he is. If you want that money pouch, you're going to have to get it yourself."

"What are you buttin' into this for?" Loomis asked. "It ain't your money."

"It isn't yours either."

"Yeah, well, it's goin' to be mine, soon as I get my hands on it," Loomis said. He put

20

his gun away and started toward the driver.

"Take another step toward that money bag and I'll kill you," Falcon said.

"What?" Loomis said in surprise. He barked what might have been a laugh. "I'll give you this, mister. You got a lot of gumption, bracing us without so much as a gun."

"Oh, I have a gun," Falcon said easily. "It's in my holster, just like yours is. And yours, and yours," he added, pointing first to Tate, then to the albino and Strayhorn.

"Maybe you didn't notice, mister, but my gun ain't in my holster," one of the other men said.

"What's your name?" Falcon asked.

"The name is Drew. Drew Tate." Drew smiled broadly.

"Tate, huh?" Falcon said. He nodded toward Loomis Tate. "Would you two be brothers?"

Drew smiled. "Yep. I see that you've heard of me."

"Can't say as I have," Falcon replied.

Drew looked shocked, and a little chagrined, that Falcon had not heard of him. Actually, Falcon had heard of him, but it was part of his strategy to let Drew think that he hadn't.

"What do you mean you ain't never heard of me?" Drew asked in consternation. With his left hand, he reached up and preened his mustache. "Why, I've kilt me seven men," Drew said. "Faced 'em down, man to man."

"Is that a fact?" Falcon said. "And did you already have your gun in your hand when you did that?"

Drew glanced down at his gun, then back at Falcon. "Oh, don't you worry none about that, mister. I'll put the gun back in my holster and we —"

"No," Falcon interrupted.

"No?" Drew said. "No what?"

"No, you won't put your gun back in your holster. If you try, I'll kill you. If you touch your mustache again, I'll kill you. If you even twitch, I'll kill you. The only thing you can do now to keep me from killing you is to drop the gun."

"Mister, are you crazy? Maybe you ain't never heard of me, but even if I was a nobody, there's two of us holdin' a gun on you, and you don't even have a gun in your hand," Drew said.

"You *are* a nobody," Falcon said calmly.

Drew's eyes narrowed. "Mister, you are just beggin' to get yourself kilt, aren't you."

"Drop the gun or make your play now," Falcon said.

"Shoot 'im, Drew, shoot 'im!" Loomis

shouted.

Drew moved his thumb to pull back the hammer, but he never made it. Before his thumb even reached the hammer, Falcon's gun was in his hand. Falcon pulled the trigger and a finger of fire spat out into the gray, wet morning. The bullet plunged into Drew's chest, causing a red mist to spray out from the entry wound.

Drew stood there just for a second, his face registering more shock than fear or pain. He turned toward Loomis.

"Big brother, he's kilt me," he said in a strained voice.

Drew let his pistol spin forward around his trigger finger, so that the barrel was pointing down and the pistol butt pointing up. He looked down at the hole in his chest, then fell back into a mud puddle, where he lay on his back, with rain falling into his open, but sightless, eyes.

"Don't shoot! Don't shoot!" Logan shouted, dropping his gun and putting his hands up.

"Logan, you cowardly son of bitch, shoot him!" Loomis shouted angrily. Loomis started for his own gun, but stopped before he even touched it when he saw that Falcon was now pointing his gun at him.

"Drop your gunbelt," Falcon ordered.

"And tell that pasty-faced son of a bitch and the fur ball with him to do the same thing. Then, all of you, put your hands up," Falcon ordered.

Reluctantly, Loomis and the others did as Falcon ordered.

"Billy, get the stage hooked up and take these good folks on into town," Falcon said.

"What about you?" Billy asked.

"Send the sheriff out here with his Black Maria to pick up his prisoners. I'll ride back with them."

"Yes, sir," Billy said. He looked at his passengers, all of whom were registering some degree of shock over the events of the morning.

"You folks get on back inside where it's warm and dry," Billy said. "I'll call you soon as the team's hitched."

"I'll give you a hand," Gulley offered.

"What about us?" Loomis asked. "Ain't you goin' to get us out of the rain?"

"You can wait in the barn," Falcon said.

CHAPTER TWO

Sheriff W. A. Smith closed the cell door, then locked it. Logan, the albino, and Strayhorn went meekly to the bunks and sat down, but Loomis remained standing, just inside the bars.

"Prison didn't hold me before, Sheriff," Loomis snarled. "What makes you think it's going to hold me this time?"

"Oh, it won't hold you," Sheriff Smith said.

"Ha!" Loomis said, laughing. "So, you don't think so either, huh? Well, maybe you ain't as dumb as you look."

"You won't be going to prison," Smith said. "We'll hang you right here in Colorado Springs."

"Hang me? Hang me for what?"

"I'm sure there are a lot of reasons to hang you. But I knew Ben Jackson. We served some in the army together, and he was a good man. Fact is, I figure he saved my life more'n once. So, I'm goin' to take particular pleasure in hangin' you for killin' ole Ben."

"I didn't kill 'im," Loomis said. "The albino killed him."

"Loomis, you squealin' son of a bitch!" the albino shouted angrily.

"Oh, don't worry," the sheriff said. "The albino will hang as well. As a matter of fact, all of you will hang, because in the eyes of the law, it doesn't matter which one of you done the actual killin'. You was all a part of it."

"That ain't right!" Loomis shouted. "That ain't no way right."

"It's a little late for you to be worryin' about what's right and what's wrong, ain't it?" the sheriff said. "Now, you folks just make yourselves comfortable back here. You won't have to stay for too long. The judge will be comin' through next week. He'll try you on Thursday and, like as not, you'll all four be dead come sunrise on Saturday."

"What about MacCallister? He killed our pard in cold blood," Loomis said. "We all seen 'im do it. You goin' to try him as well?"

"As far as I'm concerned, he just saved the county the cost of a rope," the sheriff said. "I'll have supper brought back to you in a little bit."

"Supper? We ain't had our dinner yet."

26

"Oh, didn't I tell you? The county is trying to save money, so you'll only be eatin' twice a day while you're stayin' with us. Though, if it was up to me, I wouldn't feed you anything. You're all going to be dead in a few days anyway, and there's no way you could starve to death between now and then. It would save the county the cost of feedin' you."

The sheriff turned and started back toward the front of the jail, chased by the challenging bellow of Loomis Tate.

"I ain't hangin'! Do you hear that, Sheriff? I ain't hangin'!"

Sheriff Smith closed the door to the back half of the jail, then saw Falcon MacCallister sitting on a bench, reading the newspaper. Smith had been surprised when the stagecoach driver told him that MacCallister had captured Loomis Tate and his entire band when they attempted to hold up the stage. But what had really shocked him was the driver's description of the gunfight between MacCallister and Drew Tate.

According to the driver, Drew, who had already built up quite a reputation as a fast gun, had his gun in his hand, while Falcon's gun was still in its holster. And yet, Falcon drew his gun and killed Drew before Drew could pull back the hammer.

Nobody is that fast, are they? the sheriff asked himself.

He stood for just a moment, looking at Falcon before he approached him. He knew that at one time there was paper out on Falcon MacCallister. It came out shortly after Falcon went on a killing spree, avenging the death of his wife and pa. But the killing was clearly justified, and the paper had all been withdrawn and MacCallister cleared of all charges.

That was good. The last thing Sheriff Smith wanted was to try and arrest Falcon MacCallister.

Realizing that the sheriff had been staring at him for some time, Falcon looked up in question.

"Is there anything wrong?" Falcon asked.

"No, no," the sheriff answered quickly, chastising himself for staring so long. No matter which side of the law he was on, Falcon MacCallister was not a man you wanted to make nervous. "I was just thinking, that's all."

"What were you thinking about?"

"Well, sir, I know there is a reward for Loomis Tate and his brother, Drew," Sheriff Smith said. "And I wouldn't be surprised if there isn't a reward for the others."

"A reward, huh?"

"Yes, sir, and unless I miss my guess, it'll be a pretty good reward. Looks like you earned yourself a payday."

"I don't want the money."

"What do you mean, you don't want the money? It's goin' to be paid. What do you plan to do with it?"

"If there is a reward, give it to charity," Falcon said.

"What charity?"

"I don't know. Do you have an orphanage here in Colorado Springs? A children's home, or something like that?"

The sheriff nodded. "Yes, of course we do," he answered. "And that is an excellent idea. You're a good man, Mr. MacCallister."

"Call me Falcon," Falcon said. Holding up the newspaper he was reading, he pointed to an advertisement that ran down the right hand side of the front page.

BROADMOOR DAIRY
The Oldest Dairy in Colorado Springs

Baby cries for it.
Relatives sigh for it.
Old folks demand it.
All the wise ones get it.
Daddy pays for it.
Mother prays for it.

Others crave it.
Only a few don't get it.
Remember, it pays to buy . . .

Broadmoor Milk and Cream
The Purest and the Best

"This would be James Pourtales, I take it?" Falcon said, pointing to the ad.

"Yes," the sheriff said. He sighed. "I think James would have been much better off to stick with the dairy business. This new thing of his is going to bankrupt him, I fear."

"You're talking about the Broadmoor Casino?"

"Not just the Broadmoor. He's also digging a lake, and building homes for the wealthy."

"Building homes for the wealthy? Not the poor, but the wealthy?"

"Yes, he's calling it the Cheyenne Lake and Land Improvement Company," Sheriff Smith said. "So far, he has put two hundred and forty acres of good dairy farmland, as well as nine thousand dollars of his own money, into it."

"That would explain why he was shipping so much money by stage," Falcon said. "I was wondering what he wanted with such a large amount."

30

"Yes, well, he ought to be particularly grateful to you for saving his money for him. If you have any favors you are wanting to ask of him, I'd say now would be the time," the sheriff said.

Falcon shook his head. "Nope, can't think of anything I'd want from him."

"But you came here just to see him, right?"

"Yep."

"Why?"

"Curious, I guess. He contacted me and said he wanted to discuss a business proposition. I just came to see what it was all about. You don't need me for anything else, do you?" Falcon nodded toward the back of the jail. "I mean, about the prisoners?"

"No, though before you leave town, if you are serious about giving the reward money to the orphanage, I'd like you to drop by and sign something saying that."

"All right," Falcon said. He started toward the door, but just as he reached it, the sheriff called out to him.

"Falcon?"

Falcon turned back toward the sheriff. "Yes?"

"That's a fine thing you're doin', donatin' the reward money to charity like that. I'll be sure and let 'em know where it came from."

"Tell them it came from Ben Jackson," Falcon said.

The sheriff paused for a second, then nodded. "Ben Jackson, yeah," he said. "Yeah, ole Ben's got no family, so this will be a way for folks to remember him. I thank you for that."

Falcon touched the brim of his hat, then stepped outside.

"I'll get you for this, MacCallister!" Loomis shouted just as Falcon was leaving the jail. "Do you hear me? I'll get you for this, if it's the last thing I do!"

Loomis's voice was so loud and evil-sounding that it frightened some of the people who were passing by on the street out front.

Falcon was waiting in the lobby of the hotel when he saw someone come in, then stand just inside the door as if looking for someone. The man had neatly combed hair, a high forehead, wire-rimmed glasses with narrow lenses, an expansive mustache, and a neatly trimmed beard. He was wearing a dark blue suit with a tie and a white shirt with turned-up collar.

Falcon got up from the sofa and walked toward him.

"Would you be Count Pourtales?" he asked.

The man smiled. "I would be if we were in Germany," he said, speaking English clearly, but with a pronounced German accent. "Here, I am just James Pourtales. May I take it that you are Mr. MacCallister?"

"Call me Falcon," Falcon said, extending his hand.

James shook it.

"The actors, Andrew and Rosanna Mac-Callister," Pourtales said. "I am told they are your brother and sister. Is that right?"

"Yes," Falcon said. "I'm their brother. Do you know them?"

Pourtales shook his head. "I've never met them, but I have seen them perform, both in my own country and here in America, in New York," he said. "They are positively brilliant. You must be very proud of them."

"I am proud of them," he said. "But I must confess that I am surprised you know that they are my brother and sister. We don't exactly have the same circle of friends or social contacts."

"I make it a point to find out all I can about people who interest me. And you interest me, Mr. MacCallister. In fact, I find your entire family fascinating."

"I do have some interesting people in my

family, all right," Falcon confessed.

"Come," Pourtales invited. "I have a carriage out front. I'll take you to the Broadmoor, where we can discuss business."

"I have to confess, James, I'm very curious about the business you want to discuss. That's what brought me here."

"Business is best discussed over a fine meal," Pourtales said.

A Victorian carriage was parked in front of the hotel, its driver sitting on the seat holding the reins of a matching pair of chestnuts. Climbing into the carriage, Pourtales gave the signal, and the driver snapped the reins against the back of the team. The team moved out sharply and they proceeded down Cascade Avenue, the gravel hardpacked from a recent rolling.

Pourtales had a pipe clamped in one side of his mouth, and he tamped down the tobacco, then lit it, the aromatic smoke drifting by the curved arms of his full mustache.

He continued his conversation as if there had been no break.

"Back to your family," he said. "The most fascinating of all, of course, was your father, Jamie Ian MacCallister, one of only two survivors from the battle at the Alamo. He and your mother, Kate, pushed deep into uncharted territory that would one day be called Colorado. There, he discovered a long, wide valley, nestled between towering mountains, with dark, rich dirt, fed by a wide, deep stream, and lush with timber.

"Today that is known as MacCallister Valley, and since James fathered nine children, a whole brood of blond-haired, blue-eyed children who produced another brood of blond-haired, blue-eyed children, it is literally filled with your brothers and family. They say that in that part of Colorado if one shakes a tree, a MacCallister will fall out. Am I correct so far?"

Falcon chuckled. "It's like I'm at a testimonial dinner," he said.

Pourtales laughed as well. "Then, let me continue. I never saw your father, but people say that you are the spitting image of him, not just in looks, but in the way you are: a gunfighter, a gambler, a skilled tracker, a solitary hunter, a formidable foe, a valuable friend, and a man with a strong core of right and wrong. That is why you risked your life to save my money."

Now, Pourtales's unabashed praise was beginning to make Falcon uncomfortable, so he coughed and made a joking comment.

"You'd think I was running for governor

or something."

"You would make a very good governor, but forgive me, my friend," James said. "It was not my intention to embarrass you. I just wanted you to know that I know who and what you are. Enjoy your ride through Colorado Springs. I'll be quiet until we reach our destination."

As the carriage turned in through a gate, Falcon was surprised to see a lake, placed right in the center of the mesa, with several roads radiating out from it. A dam that ran along the eastern edge of the lake provided visual evidence as to how the lake was formed.

"The lake is three hundred feet wide by fifteen hundred feet long," Pourtales explained. "As I develop the property, every house will have a nice view of the lake. And of course you see here . . ."

As if responding perfectly to the timing of Pourtales's comment, the carriage made a turn so that they were heading directly for a very large building.

"The Broadmoor Casino," Pourtales continued.

The building was a two-story wooden structure with a white colonnade across the front, as well as large, arched windows. The porch, which encircled the top floor, also created a covered walkway on the ground floor.

"You can't tell from this perspective," Pourtales said, "but my guests can enjoy the promenade to view the dramatic scenery to the east. And the back of the top floor faces out over the lake where there is a boathouse that allows small trips out onto the water."

A grassy berm in front of the building had the word BROADMOOR spelled out in flowering plants.

The carriage let them out in front of the building, and Pourtales led Falcon inside. The interior was designed with simple elegance. The large entrance hall was paneled with dark oak. Two staircases led to the second floor. The bar and gaming rooms were to the left of the entrance along with a spacious area for billiards. The ladies' salon and kitchens were to the right of the entrance, and on the upper floor, the stairways opened directly into the ballroom, where concerts could be held. Pourtales led Falcon upstairs.

"This is what I want to talk to you about," Pourtales said, taking in the ballroom with a sweep of his hand.

"You want to talk about this room?" Falcon asked.

"Yes. I believe I could put in seats enough

to hold one thousand people quite comfortably," Pourtales said. "What do you think?"

The room was exceptionally large, perhaps one of the largest rooms Falcon had ever seen.

"I suppose you could," he said.

"And with special trains put on to bring visitors to Colorado Springs, I believe I could fill it for at least ten nights. If I charged five dollars per ticket, and filled it to capacity for ten nights, I would gross fifty thousand dollars." Pourtales smiled broadly. "More than enough to pay off the debt on this place."

"Five dollars for a ticket is pretty expensive," Falcon said. "What sort of show could you have that would warrant such a charge?"

An exceptionally pretty young woman appeared then.

"Count Pourtales, dinner is ready for you and your guest," she said.

"Thank you, Louise," Pourtales said. As she walked away, Pourtales looked over at Falcon. "I apologize for her calling me Count," he said. "But I've found that, for business purposes, it does give me a certain élan."

"I understand," Falcon said.

The table was elegantly set with shimmering china, glistening crystal, and shining silver. Dinner was roast beef, roasted potatoes, green beans, rolls, and apple pie.

It was over apple pie and coffee that Pourtales finally got around to making his proposal.

"I want you to see if you can get Andrew and Rosanna MacCallister to come here and give a show in this place," he said.

"Oh, James, I don't know," Falcon said.

"Wouldn't you like to see them again? Don't you think your family would enjoy seeing them again? I would have you and your entire family as my special guests. You would all get royal treatment, have the best seats, and enjoy elegant meals and comfortable rooms. And I'm sure that Andrew and Rosanna would enjoy a trip back to the place of their childhood."

"I admit that I would like to see them come back," Falcon said. "But their schedule is always so filled."

"That isn't a problem," Pourtales said. "They merely have to add the Broadmoor to their performance schedule, that's all. Trust me, I am willing to make it well worth their while."

"What, exactly, are you willing to pay to make it worth their while?"

"Thirty percent of everything that the show makes," Pourtales offered.

"Fifty percent," Falcon countered.

"Thirty-five," Pourtales said.

"Fifty."

Pourtales chuckled and shook his head. "That's not the way you do it. You are supposed to say forty-five, and I'll counter with forty."

"Fifty percent," Falcon repeated.

Pourtales nodded. "All right," he said. "If you can get them to come here, it will be worth half of whatever I make."

"That is the big question," Falcon replied. "*If* I can get them. But I'll see what I can do."

CHAPTER THREE

Ben Jackson had been a popular man in Colorado Springs and because of this, on Thursday the courtroom was filled.

"Hear ye, hear ye, hear ye, this court will now come to order, the Honorable Judge E. A. Colburn presiding. All rise."

There was the scrape of chairs and the rustle of pants, petticoats, and skirts as the spectators in the courtroom stood. A spittoon rang as one male member of the gallery made a last-second, accurate expectoration of his tobacco quid.

Judge Colburn was a small man, but with a manner that was much larger than his size, thus making his presence immediately felt. He moved to the bench with authority, fixed a commanding gaze over the gallery, then sat down.

"Be seated."

Before the trial even began, Eli Crader, the court-appointed defense attorney, objected to having all four men tried at the same time, but Judge Colburn denied the objection.

The prosecuting attorney was C. E. Stubbs, and he called his first witness.

"Your name is Billy McClain, and you were the driver of the stage on the day the murder took place, is that right?" Stubbs asked.

"Yes, sir."

"And the gentleman who was murdered was who?"

"Ben Jackson, my shotgun guard."

"Why was he murdered?"

"Objection, Your Honor," Crader shouted. "Calls for speculation."

"Sustained."

"Withdraw my question, Your Honor," Stubbs said. He paused for a moment, then asked another question. "Were you carrying anything of value that day?"

"Yes, sir. We was carryin' ten thousand dollars for Mr. Pourtales."

"Did Loomis Tate, his brother Drew, and their associates attempt to rob you?"

"Yes, sir, and they would have, too, but Mr. MacCallister stopped them."

"When was the last time you saw Ben Jackson alive?"

"Well, sir, we had coffee that mornin';

then, while the passengers was havin' their breakfast, Ben went out to the barn to harness the team."

"And when was the next time you saw him?"

"When the albino and the redhead" — Billy pointed to Michaels and Strayhorn — "drug him out of the barn."

"Was he dead then?"

"Yes."

"Thank you, no further questions. Your witness, Counselor," Stubbs said to Crader.

Crader was a young man who had only recently begun the practice of law. He approached the witness.

"You said that Mr. Jackson was your shotgun guard," Crader began. "Would you also say he was your friend?"

"Yes, sir, he was."

"Was he a close friend?"

"My closest friend," Billy answered.

"Is it fair to say, Mr. McClain, that you would like some revenge for his death?"

"You're damn right I would like some revenge."

"So, in order to get that revenge, is it possible that you might enhance your story?"

Billy looked puzzled. "I don't know what you mean by enhance."

"Make your story strong enough to convince the jury that my clients are guilty," Crader explained.

"Hell, the sons of bitches *are* guilty," Billy said.

There was a ripple of laughter through the court, and Judge Colburn rapped his gavel once. Once was all that was required.

"No, sir, Mr. McClain, it is not for you to decide whether or not the defendants are guilty," Crader chastised. He pointed to the jury box. "That is something these twelve gentlemen must decide. Now, you told the court that you saw Mr. Michaels and Mr. Strayhorn drag Mr. Jackson's body out of the barn. But did you see anyone kill Mr. Jackson?"

"Well, yeah, I seen 'em kill Ben," Billy said. "That's what I been tellin' you."

"You're lyin'," Loomis called from the defense table. "You wasn't even in the barn when we kilt him."

The gallery laughed at Loomis's outburst, and Crader winced. This time, it took several raps of the judge's gavel before the defense attorney could continue his cross-examination.

"I put it to you again, Mr. McClain. Did you actually see any of these men kill Mr. Jackson?"

"Well, no, I mean, not if you're goin' to

put it that way. But I did see them —"

The lawyer held up his hand to stop Billy.

"Thank you, no further questions."

"But they done it," Billy said. "Hell, you just now heard Loomis say that they done it."

"Your Honor, please instruct the witness," Crader said.

"You are excused, Mr. McClain. Say nothing more unless you are asked."

Billy nodded, then glared over at the defense table as he stepped down from the witness chair.

After all the witnesses were called and examined, Colburn invited the lawyers to present their summations. Crader was first.

Crader walked over to address the jury, but was silent for several seconds before he began his summation.

"I feel a little like someone who has been ordered to sit in a poker game and play a hand that has already been dealt," he said. "It is not an easy hand to play, and if this really was poker, I would fold. But this is real life, and I can't fold. I am the court-appointed defense attorney for these men and I am honor-bound to do the best job for them that I can possibly do."

He paused again; then he raised his finger in admonition.

"But you, gentlemen of the jury, are bound by that same code of honor. If there is the slightest doubt in your mind as to whether or not my clients killed Mr. Jackson, then you must acquit them. Now, you heard Mr. Tate's outcry during my cross-examination of Mr. McClain.

"It might seem to you that Mr. Tate convicted himself by his words, but I submit to you that it was no more than a disoriented outcry upon hearing McClain say something that he knew was not true.

"McClain first stated that he had witnessed the killing; then, he recanted that statement and said that what he had witnessed was Mr. Jackson's body being dragged from the barn.

"Without an eyewitness who can testify that he *actually saw* the act of murder, then we have nothing more than speculation as to who killed Ben Jackson, or even how he died. For all we know, he could have been kicked by a horse, and my clients seized upon that opportunity as a means of extorting the money.

"Yes, I will grant you that there may have been *intent* to commit robbery, but no robbery was committed, and we aren't trying for robbery anyway. We are trying for murder and, with no actual eyewitnesses to the event, you cannot, in good conscience, find my clients guilty. Thank you for your patience."

Nervously running his hand through his hair, Crader returned to his chair.

"Prosecution, your summation," Judge Colburn called.

Stubbs stood, but did not approach the jury. "Your Honor, gentlemen of the jury, ladies and gentlemen of the gallery . . ."

"Mr. Stubbs, you know better than to address the gallery," Colburn interrupted.

"I beg your pardon, Your Honor, and I withdraw my salutation to the gallery. But before I begin my own summation, I would like to congratulate my young and most worthy opponent." Stubbs looked over at Crader. "As you said, Mr. Crader, you were dealt a very difficult hand, and you played it brilliantly. Brilliantly, sir, and my hat is off to you."

Stubbs made a small bow toward Crader, who nodded back.

Stubbs then turned his attention to the jury. "But as brilliant as my opponent was, he was not only dealt a bad hand, he was dealt a losing hand. It is obvious to anyone with any degree of reason that his clients committed this murder. It's not necessary that there be an actual eyewitness to the murder. It is only necessary that there be a preponderance of evidence to enable you to feel, beyond any reasonable doubt, that these men murdered, or were complicit in the murder of, Ben Jackson.

"The evidence and testimony presented here today will make that finding very easy for you.

"I rest my case."

To no one's surprise, the jury found Tate, Logan, Michaels, and Strayhorn guilty.

Less than an hour after Judge Colburn had entered the courtroom, the four men stood convicted for capital crimes.

"Bailiff, would you position the prisoners before the bench for sentencing, please?" Judge Colburn asked.

"Yes, Your Honor."

The four men were brought before the bench. Though Logan, Michaels, and Strayhorn stood with their heads bowed contritely, Loomis Tate stared defiantly at the judge.

"Get it over with, old man," Loomis said. "I ain't got all day." He giggled at his own joke.

"Loomis Tate, Matthew Logan, Ron Michaels, and Ken Strayhorn, I hereby order the sheriff to lead you to the gallows at ten of the clock on Saturday morning where the four of you will be hanged by the neck until you are dead, dead, dead, and dead."

CHAPTER FOUR

Pourtales's carriage stopped in front of the Denver and Rio Grande depot. Built of brick, the depot was one of the more impressive-looking buildings in town. It had a red-tiled roof with dormers and a cupola on top from which someone could observe the train traffic on the eight sets of tracks that made up the yard.

"I appreciate you going to New York for me," Pourtales said.

"It's not that much of an imposition," Falcon said. "I will enjoy having the opportunity to see my brother and sister again. And I've been to New York before. It is an interesting town."

"Indeed it is," Pourtales said. "I must admit, though, that I'm somewhat surprised you aren't going to stay in town for the hanging this Saturday."

Falcon shook his head. "I've seen men hanged," he said. "It's not something

I enjoy."

"Nor do I," Pourtales said. "But Ben Jackson was a very popular man here, and I think many are going, just to satisfy themselves that justice is done."

"And almost as many just to see the spectacle," Falcon replied.

"I can't argue with that," Pourtales said. "But it's nothing new. The Romans made an art of it with their games in the Colosseum."

The carriage driver returned, then gave a ticket to Falcon.

"Your luggage has been checked through, Mr. MacCallister. It'll be in New York when you are."

"If it doesn't get on the wrong train in Denver, and wind up in San Francisco or New Orleans," Falcon joked.

"You'll arrive in New York when?" Pourtales asked.

"Next Wednesday evening," Falcon said.

"Less than a week. My, we do live in a marvelous age."

"I'll say. It took my pa three months to get out here," Falcon said.

They heard the sound of a whistle, and Pourtales turned in his seat to see the glow of a distant headlamp.

"Here it comes," he said.

Falcon nodded, then climbed down from the carriage before reaching back up to shake Pourtales's hand. "I'll send you a wire as soon as I talk to them," he said.

"I hope they will come," Pourtales said. "But whether they do or not, it has been an honor to have met you."

"Likewise," Falcon said.

By now the train was rolling into the yard and the sound of the puffing engine was quite audible. The engineer blew the whistle, then rang the bell, and as the train drew closer, Falcon could hear the hissing of steam and air, and the squeal of metal on metal as the brakes were applied. With a final wave, he started toward the platform, arriving at about the same time as the train.

Passing a paperboy, Falcon bought a copy of the *Gazette* and took it on the train. There would be no Pullman cars available until he left Denver. The paper, he thought, would help him pass the time.

FOUR MEN TO BE HURLED INTO ETERNITY!

Notorious Loomis Tate One of the Men.

His Brother Drew Killed by Falcon MacCallister.

SPECIAL TO THE GAZETTE: In a trial presided over by the Honorable E. A. Colburn, Judge of El Paso County, and brilliantly prosecuted by Mr. C. E. Stubbs, the fates of Loomis Tate, Ron Michaels, Ken Strayhorn, and Matthew Logan were placed before a jury of twelve men, good and true.

Despite a spirited defense offered by young Eli Crader, all four men were found guilty and sentenced to be hanged on Saturday next, at the morning hour of ten. A fifth member of the nefarious gang, one Drew Tate, known for his skill with a pistol, was spared from hanging, because he made the mistake of challenging Falcon MacCallister to a gunfight. Drew was dispatched on the spot.

By the time Falcon finished with the newspaper, the train was well out of town and traveling at the speed of more than twenty-five miles per hour. Falcon leaned back in his seat, put his knees on the seat in front of him, then tipped his hat down over his eyes. He had better get used to train travel. He had almost a week of it in front of him.

Back in Colorado Springs the next morning, Matthew Logan paced back and forth in the cell that he was sharing with the other three condemned men. At one point he stopped his pacing and just stared straight ahead at the block wall.

"What are you tryin' to do, Logan, stare a hole in the wall?" Strayhorn asked.

The albino chuckled. "Maybe he thinks he can stare a hole in the wall and we can all just walk through it."

"Shut up, Michaels," Logan said angrily. "If it wasn't for you, we wouldn't be about to get our necks stretched. You're the one should be gettin' hung, not us."

The sound of the pulley straining with the sand-weight floated across the town square outside the cell and in through the tiny barred window. As the weight slammed down against the trapdoor, Logan jumped.

"What are they doin' that for?" he asked in a tight voice. "That sound — it's drivin' me crazy!"

"You ought to be glad they're testin' it

out like that, Logan," Strayhorn said. "If they don't get ever'thing just right, why, like as not you'll just hang there and choke to death."

"Or else, it'll jerk your head clean off your body," the albino said. His cackle was like laughter from hell.

The albino put his hand to his neck. "I never thought I'd be hung. I figured I might get shot someday, but I never thought I'd get hung."

"We ain't been hung yet," Loomis said. He was lying on the bunk with his arm across his eyes, and this was the first thing he had said in a long time.

"Yeah, but we're goin' to be, and I wish they'd just go ahead and do it and get it over with," Logan said.

Outside, they tested the gallows again, and the men in the cell heard the trapdoor fall open and the sandbag hit the ground with a violent thud.

"Stop, damn you, stop!" Logan shouted. He put his hands over his ears.

The albino laughed again, a dry, skeletal laugh.

Any public hanging drew the morbidly curious, but because four were to be executed, this one became an event. On the morning appointed, visitors came from far and wide to see the spectacle, so many that the Denver and Rio Grande Railroad had to add additional trains to accommodate the passenger load. As a result, there were almost as many visitors as there were residents of the town, and nearly all were gathered on the square on Saturday morning.

The gallows stood in the center of town, its grisly shadow stretching under the morning sun. It was just past nine, and the hanging wasn't scheduled to take place until ten. But the square was already filled, though people continued to crowd in, jostling for position.

Several hundred people were gathered around the gallows, men in suits and work clothes, women in dresses and bonnets, and children darting about in the crowd. A few enterprising vendors passed through the crowd selling lemonade, beer, and bear claws. An itinerant preacher stood at the side of the gallows, taking advantage of the situation to deliver a fiery harangue to the crowd.

"In a few moments four men are going to be hung — sent to meet their Maker with blood on their hands and sin in their hearts."

He waggled his finger at the crowd. "And hear this now! Them four lost souls is going to be cast into hell because there ain't a one of 'em what's got down on his knees and prayed to the Lord for forgiveness of his sins.

"It's too late for them, brothers 'n' sisters. They are doomed to the fiery furnaces of hell, doomed to writhe in agony forever!"

Some of those who were close enough to hear the preacher shivered involuntarily at his powerful imagery and looked toward the gallows. One or two of them touched their necks fearfully, and a few souls, perhaps weak on willpower, sneaked a drink from a bottle.

"It's too late for them, but it's not too late for you! Repent! Repent now, I say, for the wages of sin is death and eternal perdition!"

The preacher's voice carried well, and could be heard by the four men in the holding cell. From time to time, first one face, then another, would appear in the window, look out through the bars at the crowd, and then disappear. Some of the older children climbed up on a box and looked in through the window from outside.

"Get away from there!" Logan shouted at the face of a young boy in the window.

"Mister, what's it feel like to know you're a'fixin' to die?" the boy asked.

"Get away from there now, damn you!" Logan screamed, running toward the window.

Logan's scream had the desired effect, because the boy ducked away out of sight.

"Logan, will you, for God's sake, sit down? You're as nervous as a whore in church," Loomis growled.

"Don't you think I have a right to be nervous? They're about to hang us out there."

"Yeah, that's what they say," Loomis replied, his voice agonizingly calm.

"Don't this mean nothin' to you?" Logan asked. "How come you're not worried about it?"

"What good's worryin' do?" Loomis replied.

There was the sound of keys, rattling in the lock of the door. "Oh! They're coming for us!" Logan said, his voice breaking with panic.

Loomis sat up on the side of his bunk and looked toward the door. He smiled broadly as he saw someone fitting a key into the lock. The man was tall and slim, with an oversized handlebar mustache.

"Hello, Kelly," he said. "You sure as hell

took your time gettin' here."

"This is the first chancet I've had," Kelly said.

"Boys, this here is my other brother, Kelly Tate," Loomis said.

"Your brother?" Logan asked. He laughed. "He sure as hell don't look nothin' like you."

"Who'd want to look like that ugly bastard?" Kelly teased, and the others laughed.

"So, that's why you wasn't worried, huh? 'Cause you've got another brother?"

"Yeah, I figured he'd come get me out," Loomis said.

"Am I ever glad to meet you!" Logan said. He put his hand to his neck. "I thought we was goin' to hang for sure.

"We better hurry," Kelly said. "If someone finds the guard with his head bashed in, they're going to know something is going on."

"You got the horses?"

"Yeah, they're down at the livery."

"You couldn't get 'em no closer'n that?" Loomis scolded.

"Not without anyone getting suspicious. But don't worry, there's so many people out there now, we could walk right through the middle of the crowd butt-naked and nobody'd even notice."

"Come on," Logan said, "let's go."

59

"Not yet," Loomis replied, heading toward the office.

"What are you doing?" Logan asked. "Come on, we've got to get out of here before anyone else shows up."

"Don't you think it would be good if we had our guns?"

"Oh. Yeah," Logan said. "Yeah, I guess so."

Kelly was already armed, though there was blood on the butt of his pistol as a result of it being used as a club against the guard. He went over to the drinking-water pail and dipped the pistol into it, then used a towel to clean it off while the other four found their guns and began strapping them on. After the albino strapped on his own gun, he walked over to the deputy on the floor, then got his pistol as well.

"What are you doing?" Strayhorn asked.

"It never hurts to have a second gun," the albino said.

That was when Loomis saw some paper and a pencil.

"Wait a minute," he said, picking up the pencil.

"What are you going to do?" the albino asked. "Write a letter?"

"Yeah, sort of," Loomis said.

TO FALCON MACALESTER

I AM GOING TO GIT EVIN WITH YOU
FOR KILLIN MY BROTHER LIKE YOU
DUN JUST YOU WAIT AND SEE.
                                    LOOMIS TATE

"Put my name on there, too," Kelly said.

"I do that, folks will know you was the one helped us escape," Loomis said. "And they'll figure you're the one who killed the guard."

Kelly chuckled. "Hell, Loomis, ain't none of us goin' to get out of this alive anyway. Put my name on it like I said."

Nodding, Loomis marked out the I AM and wrote in WE ARE, then added KELLY TATE under his own name.

The five men stepped out into the alley behind the jail, then walked down to next street and joined the crowd.

"Hey, Jake, is it true whenever someone gets hung that their neck stretches out?" they heard someone in the crowd ask.

"Yep, it's true all right," Jake answered. "I've seen it myself."

"Four of 'em. Whoowee, four of 'em. By damn, this'll be somethin' I can tell my grandkids someday."

Logan's face flushed in anger, and he

started toward the two men, but Loomis grabbed him and pulled him back.

"Maybe you got no more sense than to get yourself hung, but I don't intend to let you get *me* hung," Loomis hissed angrily. "Don't say nothin' to nobody. Just keep goin' till we get to the horses."

Logan didn't answer, but he did nod. Five minutes later they were at the edge of town, having walked their horses through the city. It was one of the most difficult things Logan had ever done, because every muscle in his body screamed out for him to run. To his own surprise, he managed to stay calm. It was not until they mounted, and rode slowly for about a mile, that Loomis gave them the word.

"All right, boys," he said. "Let's go like a bat out of hell."

The five riders broke into a gallop.

Even as Loomis and the others were putting distance between themselves and Colorado Springs, Sheriff Smith was stepping into the office.

He didn't see the guard, and from the moment he stepped into the office, he had a strange feeling. It wasn't anything he could put his finger on, but it just didn't seem right.

"Leroy?" he called.

There was no answer.

"Leroy," he called again. "Where are you?" he called. "It's time to get the prisoners ready."

Sheriff Smith had left the front door open, and now a freshening breeze blew it shut with a slam. Startled, Smith drew his pistol and whirled around, only to see that the door had blown shut.

"Damn, Leroy," Sheriff Smith called, putting his pistol back in his holster. "Will you come out here? You've got me drawing on doors now."

Seeing the door that led back to the cells open, Sheriff Smith assumed that Leroy was back with the prisoners. He walked into the area that housed the cells, then stopped.

The cell where his prisoners had been kept was empty, the door standing wide open.

"What the hell?" he asked aloud.

"Leroy! Leroy, where are you?"

Pulling his pistol again, Sheriff Smith pushed open the back door, very slowly, and looked out into the alley.

He saw nothing.

"Leroy, are you back here?" he called. He was nursing the hope that Leroy might have found the prisoners gone and come to the alley to look for them.

Sighing when his call netted no response, Sheriff Smith returned to the front office. That was when he glanced over toward Leroy's desk again. This time, because of the angle, he saw something he hadn't seen earlier. He saw a boot sticking out from behind the desk.

"Oh, no," he said quietly. "Please, God, no."

The sheriff walked over for a closer look.

His young deputy was lying on his back behind the desk. There was a large, dark wound on top of his head, and a pool of blood spread beneath it. "Oh, Leroy," Sheriff Smith said sadly, kneeling down to check his condition.

He didn't have to put his hand on Leroy's neck to feel for a pulse. He knew, even before he touched him, that the young man was dead.

CHAPTER FIVE

Loomis Tate and the others rode hard after they left Colorado Springs, and by nightfall they were at least thirty miles away. They spent an uneasy night on the ground, then got up at first light the next morning.

"Damn, I'm hungry," Logan said. "I ain't et since breakfast in jail yesterday morning."

"There ain't none of us ate," Strayhorn said.

"I know, I was just sayin' I was hungry, is all," Logan said.

"Let's get goin'," Loomis ordered, and the five men mounted their horses and rode on.

It was no more than half an hour later that Loomis called out to the other riders.

"Hold up, hold up. My horse has gone lame."

The others looked back toward Loomis and saw that his horse was limping badly.

"Where the hell did you get these horses?"

Loomis asked.

"From the back lot of the livery," Kelly said. "I couldn't be too choosy. I had to take what I found."

"You got 'em from the back lot?" Logan asked.

"Yeah."

"Damn," Logan said. "We'll all be ridin' cripple horses soon. That's where they turn the horses out that's too old to ride anymore. I wouldn't be surprised if these horses wasn't older'n we are."

"Well, I'm sorry I couldn't bring everyone three-year-old Arabians," Kelly said.

"My brother done what he could," Loomis said. "Ain't no sense in bitchin' about it now. But we do need to get us some better horses or we're goin' to wind up afoot."

"Where do you plan to get 'em?" Strayhorn asked.

"We need to find us a ranch or a farm somewhere," Loomis said. "We'll get us some breakfast there, then take whatever horses we can find. Logan, me an' you will double up on your horse."

"Why are you doublin' up with me?" Logan complained. "Why don't you double up with Kelly? He's your brother."

Loomis pulled his pistol and pointed it at Logan. "Of course, I could just kill you and take your horse," he said.

"No, no," Logan said quickly, putting his hands up as if warding Loomis off. "You can double up with me if you want to."

"Yeah," Loomis said. "I thought you might see it that way."

With Loomis and Logan riding double, they were not able to travel as fast as they had been traveling before, but as it turned out it didn't matter, because after another mile they came upon a ranch.

"Look down there, boys," Loomis said, pointing to the ranch.

With the sun still low in the east, a soft golden light was falling upon nearly two dozen horses gamboling about in the corral.

"I do believe Christmas has come early," he said.

The Rocking R Ranch belonged to Elam Rafferty, and though it wasn't a particularly large ranch, it was successful because he had a reputation for raising exceptionally good horses that brought premium prices. It also helped that it was a small, one-man operation and didn't cost much to run.

Sue Rafferty liked this time of day best, when the air was soft and still cool and there was a freshness about everything. She saw a few dead blooms amid the colorful profusion in her flower garden, and reminded herself that she would have to do a little puttering later, when she had time.

As Sue walked down the path toward the barn, the blades of the barnyard windmill answered a breeze, turned into the wind, and began spinning. Sue continued on out to the barn to call her daughter and son in for breakfast.

Lucy, her sixteen-year-old daughter, was milking, while fourteen-year-old Jimmy was forking hay into the horses' feeding trough. She stopped just outside the barn for a moment to watch her children at work. They had grown from being underfoot to being somewhat helpful, to being almost indispensable.

"Breakfast is ready," Sue said.

"Good," Jimmy said, rubbing his hands together. "I'm so hungry that I'm near 'bout stove in."

"Sure you are," Lucy said. "Why, anybody could see that you are just wasting away."

Jimmy was a big boy for his age. He was only fourteen years old, but was already taller than his mother. And a good appetite and a lot of work had caused him to bulk up some.

"At least I'm not so skinny that I don't even throw a shadow," Jimmy teased, tossing some hay at his sister.

"Mama!" Lucy called out.

"Mama!" Jimmy mimicked.

"Jimmy, don't do that," Sue scolded. "I just washed Sis's hair last night."

"What a coward you are, running to Mama for help," Jimmy teased. "What's the matter, are you too much of a coward to fight back?"

"I'm not raising my daughter to be a common brawler," Sue said. "I wish I could say the same for you."

"What are we having for breakfast?" Jimmy asked.

"Bacon, eggs, biscuits, fried potatoes," Sue said. "You and your pa are going to be clearing some pastureland, so you'll be needing a substantial breakfast."

"I don't think I can help him today," Jimmy said. He put his hand around to the middle of his back. "I think I must have hurt my back a while ago."

Lucy reached up and flicked her brother on the earlobe, then jumped away from him as he twisted around to try and get her.

"Ha!" Lucy said. "It doesn't look to me like you have a bad back."

"You're going to help your pa today, Jimmy, and that's all there is to it," Sue said. "Now, get washed up and come on in the house for breakfast."

Sue went back into the house, carrying the pail of milk Lucy had gotten, while Lucy and Jimmy stepped over to the pump to wash up. Sue pumped the water for Jimmy as he held his hands under the spout, washing them vigorously with a bar of lye soap. Then Jimmy operated the pump handle for Lucy — stopping just as she got her hands well lathered.

"No, don't stop pumping now," Lucy said. "Can't you see that I've got soap on my hands?"

"What will you give me to pump some more water for you?" Jimmy asked.

Lucy reached up and ran her soapy hands through Jimmy's hair. "I'll give you a hard time if you don't," she said.

"Hey, stop!" Jimmy said, and laughing, he pumped the handle until her hands, and his hair, were free of soap.

They were still laughing when Jimmy pushed the door to the house open. Then they came to a complete halt as their eyes widened in confusion.

There were five strange men in the kitchen. One was short and stocky, with a bushy red beard and hair. He was standing behind their father, holding a gun to his head. Another was medium-sized, pale-skinned, with pink eyes. The albino was holding their mother down in a chair, with a knife at her throat.

A third intruder had pockmarked skin and a drooping eye. He was standing by the table eating a biscuit and bacon sandwich. The other two were standing by the back wall, almost as if they were observing what was going on, rather than participating in the unfolding drama.

"Well, now, would you lookee at what just come dragging in here," Loomis said.

"Mama, Papa, what's going on?" Lucy asked.

"Just — just do as they say and everything will be all right," Sue said, her voice quavering with fear.

"Who are these men?"

"I know who this one is," Jimmy said, pointing to the one with the droopy eye.

"You know who I am, do you, boy?" Loomis asked.

"Yes."

"How is it that you know me?"

"I seen your picture on a wanted poster oncet when I was in town. You're Loomis Tate, ain't you?"

"That's my name, all right," Loomis said. "What's your name, boy?" he asked.

"Jimmy. Jimmy Rafferty."

"Jimmy Rafferty, is it? You're a pretty smart boy, ain't you, Jimmy Rafferty?" Loomis said.

"I'm smart enough," Jimmy replied challengingly.

"Well, if there's one thing I don't need, it's a smart boy," Loomis growled. He pulled out his gun and before anyone could say a word, pulled the trigger. The gun roared, a wicked finger of flame flashed from the barrel of the gun, and a cloud of smoke billowed out over the table. The bullet hit Jimmy in the forehead and he fell back, dead before he hit the floor.

"You bastard!" Elam Rafferty yelled, shocked by what he had just seen. Surprising Strayhorn, who was supposed to be watching him, Elam jumped up from his chair and leaped onto Loomis, knocking him down. He began struggling to get the gun from Loomis.

"Get him off of me! Get him off of me!" Loomis screamed.

Strayhorn redeemed his mistake in watching his prisoner by stepping over quickly and putting the end of the gun no more than an inch away from Elam's temple. He pulled the trigger and blood and brain matter spewed from the bullet hole as Elam fell dead beside his son.

"Papa! Jimmy!" Lucy screamed. She dropped to her knees beside them and put her hands over her eyes trying desperately to deny what was before her.

"Murderers!" Jimmy's mother yelled. She tried to stand up, but the pale-faced one shoved her back down in her chair, then cut a nick in her face with the tip of his knife. A bright red stream of blood began flowing from the cut. "Oh, my God! Oh, my God!" she screamed.

Loomis, who had by now gotten up from the floor, looked over at Sue. "Shut up, woman," he ordered, "or I'll have the albino slit you open from gullet to gizzard."

Sue bit her bottom lip and trembled with terror and grief as she saw both her husband and her son lying dead on the kitchen floor.

"You, girlie, what's your name?" Loomis asked the young girl.

"My name is Lucy."

"Get up, Lucy. Get over there with your mama."

Lucy did as she was ordered; then she reached down and grabbed her mother's hand.

"Have you got 'ny money in this house?" Loomis asked.

"It's over there in the hutch," Sue said. "In the middle drawer."

Loomis went over to the hutch and opened the drawer. He saw some money there, but when he pulled it out and counted, he frowned.

"Forty dollars?" he said. "All you have is forty dollars?"

"Elam did not believe in keeping much cash in the house. He keeps all our money in the bank."

"Well, then, forty dollars and breakfast will have to do," Loomis said. "Oh, and we'll be borrowing a few horses when we leave," he added.

Kelly laughed. "Borrowing a few horses," he said. He laughed again. "Like we're goin' to bring 'em back."

"Loomis, there's somethin' else here we could use," the albino said.

"What?"

The albino looked pointedly at Lucy. "Are you a virgin?" he asked.

"What?" Lucy asked, shocked by the question.

"It's a simple question, girlie. Are you a virgin? Have you ever been with a man?"

"No! No, of course not!"

"What are you getting' at, Michaels?" Loomis asked.

"There's people in Mexico willin' to pay a lot of money for white women," he said.

74

"And they'll pay just real good for a young virgin girl."

Loomis looked at Lucy and at her mother; then he shook his head.

"No," he said. "I ain't goin' to Mexico till I deal with MacCallister."

"Whatever you say," the albino said. "I just hate to be wastin' these two women is all."

Loomis smiled, then rubbed himself.

"Oh, don't you be worryin' none about that," he said. "We ain't goin' to waste 'em," he added. He reached out and put his hand on the neck of Lucy's dress, then jerked it down, tearing it away to expose her nubile, young naked body.

"Oh, yeah," Loomis said, leering at her. "You're tittied up just real good."

"What about this woman?" the albino asked.

"We'll take our turns with both of 'em," Loomis said as he began opening his belt. "But I got first on this one."

CHAPTER SIX

Falcon remembered having read somewhere that Union Station in St. Louis was the busiest railroad hub in the entire world, with more than 25,000 passengers per day passing through the station. It was a claim he could easily believe as he stepped into the passenger ticketing and waiting room.

An enormous gaslight chandelier, hanging from a sixty-five-foot-high vaulted ceiling, dominated the Grand Hall. The floor teemed with humanity: men and women moving to or from trains, children laughing or crying. As the trains entered or departed from the great covered train shed, Falcon could feel the floor rumbling under his feet.

Falcon went to an information booth.

"Good evening, sir," one of the agents in the booth greeted said. "May I help you?"

"I'm changing trains here, going on to New York," Falcon said, showing his long row of multi-sectioned tickets. "I just want to make sure I'm on the right train at the right time."

The agent examined the tickets. "You came from Colorado Springs, I see," he said. "You are making quite a long journey."

"Yes."

"Ahh, here it is. You will board the Flying Eagle on track number twelve at eight o'clock." The agent looked up at a huge clock. "It's just after seven-thirty and you have first-class passage. They are boarding first-class passengers now, and I am sure you will find the parlor car seats much more comfortable than the hard wooden benches of the waiting room."

"Yes, I believe I would. Thanks," Falcon said, starting toward a door under a sign that read: TO TRAINS.

When Falcon stepped through the door, it was almost as if he had stepped from one world to another. Behind him was the large, domed waiting room. Before him was the great train shed with thirty-one tracks.

As the heavy trains moved in and out of the shed, Falcon could not only hear them, he could feel them in the pit of his stomach. He could smell the aroma of coal and wood smoke, and overheated bearings and gearboxes. Wisps of steam drifted through the shed, almost iridescent in the lampposts that illuminated the long, cement platforms that ran the length of the tracks between sitting trains.

Falcon found track number twelve, then showed his ticket to the conductor.

"Yes, sir," the conductor said. "You are in a Wagner Palace car, the third car back from the baggage car. It is number one-seven-six."

"Thank you," Falcon said, starting up the long, narrow, walkway between the Flying Eagle and the Chicago Limited, which was parked on the adjacent track.

Inside the Palace car, the lanterns were all at their brightest as the few privileged passengers prepared for the long trip. Falcon entered the car, passing a beautiful young woman who was trying to put a hatbox in the overhead rack. The young woman was stretching to reach it, but it was beyond her reach.

Her effort to reach the overhead rack showed every curve of her body in a way that caused Falcon to stop, just for a moment, to enjoy the view. Then, stepping up to her, he offered his help.

"Allow me," Falcon said. He smiled graciously at the lady and reached up to put the hatbox in place.

"Thank you, sir," the young woman replied.

"My pleasure, miss," Falcon said, touching the brim of his hat.

Unlike the day car he had taken out of Colorado Springs, this car was handsome and elegant in every detail. It was richly paneled inside with burled walnut and golden gilt; the seats were large and mounted on swivels to allow the passengers to enjoy the view through the window, or to turn the seats inward for conversation with other passengers. The seats also reclined for comfort during the day, but when night arrived, there were private sleeping compartments at each end of the car.

Falcon had not been in his seat for more than a few minutes when a young boy, wearing a Western Union cap, came into the car.

"Mr. MacCallister? Is there someone in here named Falcon MacCallister?" the boy called.

"I'm Falcon MacCallister," Falcon said, lifting his hand.

"I have a telegram for you, Mr. MacCallister," the boy said.

"A telegram?"

"Yes, sir, it actually come this afternoon, but it said you'd be on this train."

"All right, thanks," Falcon said, handing

79

the boy a half-dollar.

The boy smiled broadly. "Gee, thanks, mister," he said.

Falcon opened the telegram.

MR MACCALLISTER
LOOMIS TATE AND HIS GANG MUR-
DERED GUARD AND ESCAPED JAIL THIS
MORNING STOP THOUGHT YOU
SHOULD BE INFORMED OF SITUATION
STOP

JAMES POURTALES

It was midnight when the train reached Indianapolis, but Falcon left it long enough to go into the depot and send a telegram back to Pourtales. He asked the entrepreneur if he still wanted Falcon to bring his brother and sister back to perform in the Broadmoor.

The answer reached him the next day as the train paused briefly in Buffalo.

YES STOP THIS CHANGES NOTHING
STOP

Falcon arrived at Grand Central Station in New York on the evening of the sixth day of travel. He had not informed his brother and sister that he was coming to New York, and he made no effort to contact them now. Instead, he got a room in the Bixby Hotel on Broadway, bought a copy of the *New York Times,* then went to his room to relax and read the paper.

As it turned out, under the "Entertainments" Section, he saw an article about Andrew and Rosanna.

For two months now, since the start of the season, the more sophisticated playgoers in New York have enjoyed a performance that is so lavish in its staging, so rich in its orchestral presentation, and so aptly played by the actors, that no other offering is its equal.

I am talking about the play entitled *The Mulligan Guard Ball,* which has enjoyed a very successful run at the Bijou Opera House on Broadway.

Of course, *The Mulligan Guard Ball* has been presented on the New York stage before, but never with the plentitude of talent as displayed by its two principal players, Andrew and Rosanna MacCallister. Equal to Sarah Bernhardt and Edwin Booth in their thespian skills, the two MacCallisters give a performance that must be seen by any aficionado of the theater.

Such is the pity that tomorrow night will be the last night of this fine show. Any who have not seen this play, and can avail themselves of the opportunity to do so, would be well advised to take advantage of this, the last performance, not only of this company's production, but perhaps of any future production.

Falcon put the paper aside, extinguished the lantern, then laid his head on the pillow. He'd been going to contact them where they live, but after reading the paper, he had a better idea.

CHAPTER SEVEN

The message on the marquee of the Bijou Opera House advertised the performance in letters so large that even passengers in the carriages on Broadway could read it quite clearly.

LAST NIGHT! ONE PERFORMANCE ONLY!

ANDREW AND ROSANNA MacCALLISTER

~ *Starring in* ~

HARRIGAN AND HART'S "The Mulligan Guard Ball"

A colorful poster in front of the theater had a photograph of the principal players wearing the military costumes of their roles.

Hired cabs and liveried carriages disgorged patrons in front of the theater as they filed in to catch this, the very last night.

"Have you ever seen the MacCallisters?" one woman was asking another. "They are brilliant."

"Were they already in the theater when they met and married?"

"Oh, my dear, they aren't married."

"They aren't? But their names . . ."

"They are brother and sister."

"I didn't know that."

"Oh, yes, and they are from quite a colorful family. Their father was Daniel Boone, or Davy Crockett, or some such person."

"Andrew also has quite a colorful background on his own, from what I hear," another said.

"Curtain time! Five minutes until curtain time!" a young man in a maroon uniform shouted as he walked through the crowded lobby. "Curtain time! Five minutes until curtain time!"

"We'd better hurry inside."

Within moments, the lobby cleared as everyone moved quickly into the theater to claim their seats. After the noise of settling in quieted, the curtains opened to disclose the two stars standing on the stage.

The crowd applauded.

Rosanna MacCallister, wearing the ill-fitting parody of a militia uniform, was playing Kate. In character, she stepped to the middle of the stage, then, clasping her hand across her heart, emoted loudly enough to be heard by all fifteen hundred patrons.

KATE

McSweeney, what's the name of the hall the young Mulligans have hired for the ball?

Andrew MacCallister, her costar and brother, wearing a similar uniform, was playing "McSweeney." He listened attentively, then, spreading his arms wide, turned to the audience to deliver his response.

McSWEENEY

Sure'n 'tis the Harp and Shamrock, Katie m'darlin'.

KATE

I want to see the hall look nice. Will you do what I say?

McSWEENEY

Yes, sling on anything, Kate, I'm with you.

KATE

No, but fix the hall the way I want it.

Get a row of American flags on the right hand, with the Irish flags blending between them. Then get a row of wax candles on the balcony, and put a sign on it, "Look out for the drip." Get about thirty-three canaries, and some blackbirds, in cages, and hang them on the chandeliers, and give word to the leader of the band, if a Dutch tune is played the whole night, he'll not get a cent.

(laughter from the crowd)

Will you do this?

McSWEENEY
I will, you bet your life, Kate.

KATE
Come on. Do ye remember the old tune?

KATE *(singing)*
We shouldered arms
And marched
And marched away,
From Baxter Street
We marched to Avenue A.
With drums and fifes
How sweetly they did play
As we marched, marched, marched
In the Mulligan Guards.

McSWEENEY *(staggering, as if drunk)*
When we'd get home at night, boys,
The divil a wink we'd sleep;

At this, Andrew put his thumbs under his armpits, then tilted his head and winked at the audience. The audience responded with laughter, and Andrew had to wait for a moment before continuing with his song.

McSWEENEY
We'd all sit up and drink a sup
Of whiskey, strong and neat.
Then we'd all march home together,
As slippery as lard;
The solid men would all fall in,
And march in the Mulligan Guard.

Now, arm in arm, and responding to the music of the band, Andrew and Rosanna did a parody of a march around the stage. Their antics received raucous laughter from the audience.

The show revolved around two rival groups renting the same hall on the same night, and it continued for three acts of song, dance, and dialogue as the Mulligan Guard attempted to work out the problem with the Knights of Bronx.

At the conclusion of the show, Andrew

and Rosanna came together, held hands, and made a deep bow to the applauding audience. The curtains closed, then opened to the continuing applause of the audience. Andrew held out his hand to welcome the other players on stage, appearing in reverse order of their importance to the play.

The other players came out in ones and twos, until finally all were standing on the stage. Then, taking his sister's hand, Andrew stepped to the front with Rosanna for one final bow.

As the curtains closed for the final time, everyone rushed off the stage in order to get out of makeup and costumes.

"Dinner at Delmonico's?" Rosanna called to her brother as they hurried through the dim corridors backstage.

"Delmonico's it is," Andrew called back.

"Ha! If you don't watch yourself with such midnight dinners, you'll grow so fat that the oversized costume you are wearing on stage may actually fit," a man's voice called from the shadows.

"What?" Rosanna replied, stung by the words.

"Sir, how dare you make such a remark to my sister!" Andrew said in an angry, challenging voice.

"Well, she's my sister, too, Andrew,"

Falcon MacCallister replied, stepping out of the shadows with a wide smile spreading across his face.

"Falcon!" Rosanna screamed in joy. She ran to him with her arms spread wide. "Oh, what a pleasure to see you here!"

Falcon embraced and kissed his sister, then shook hands with his brother.

"How wonderful to see you!" Andrew said. Then, the expression on his face showed worry. "Oh, is anything wrong? Our family?"

"All are well," Falcon said.

Both Andrew and Rosanna heaved a sigh of relief.

"That is good news to hear," Andrew said. "But what are you doing here?"

"Can I not come to New York to visit my brother and sister?"

"Yes, yes, of course you can, anytime!" Rosanna said. Then, frowning at Andrew, she added, "Andrew, what is wrong with you? Does our little brother need a reason to come to New York?"

"Little brother?" Andrew said with a laugh. Though he was the youngest, Falcon had grown up to be the largest of the Mac-Callister clan. Towering almost six inches over Andrew, Falcon was the same size as, and many said the spitting image of, his father, Jamie Ian MacCallister.

"And of course he doesn't need an excuse," Andrew continued. "It is just that, well, quite frankly, I do not think of Falcon as being a man of the city. I believe him to be much more at home on some remote Western mountain peak than on Broadway."

"We were about to go out to eat," Rosanna said to Falcon. "Will you have dinner with us?"

"Dinner at eleven? I'm more used to supper at six than dinner at eleven. But I'll be glad to go with you. I'll have some coffee."

"And dessert," Rosanna said. "The chocolate cake at Delmonico's is delicious enough to die for."

Falcon chuckled and shook his head. "There are things I would die for, Rosanna," he said. "But I don't believe chocolate cake at Delmonico's is one of them."

"Well, then, let's just say that you will enjoy the cake," Rosanna said. "You must take dessert with us."

"You don't have to twist my arm for that," Falcon replied.

Delmonico's was on Twenty-sixth Street, north of Madison Square. The beautiful and fashionable restaurant was five stories high, with an elegant crest mounted in an arch on top. The windows were protected by awnings, as was the ground level. An ornate iron grillwork fence surrounded the restaurant, creating a place for sidewalk dining.

"Isn't it beautiful?" Rosanna asked as they stepped out of the cab. It just moved here four years ago. It used to be down on Fourteenth and Fifth."

A uniformed policeman, wearing a domed pith helmet, was standing on the corner. He nodded a greeting at the MacCallisters as they left the cab.

Two men and two women were leaving the restaurant as Falcon, his brother, and his sister started in. One of the women, recognizing Andrew and Rosanna, stopped and smiled broadly.

"Oh! You are the MacCallisters," the woman gushed. "I simply must have your autographs."

Smiling, and exchanging pleasantries with her, Andrew and Rosanna signed their autographs on a paper the woman presented, and then they went into the restaurant. There, they were greeted as old and valued customers, then escorted to a table. A few moments later, the chef himself, Allesandro Filippini, came to their table to greet them.

"This is our brother," Andrew said, indicating Falcon. "He lives in Colorado."

"Colorado. That is in the West, is it not?" Filippini asked.

"Yes, it is."

"It must be quite exciting to live in such a place."

"For our brother it is exciting," Rosanna said, "for he has performed many heroic deeds in his lifetime. In fact, he is well known for his exploits and his derring-do."

"Yes, I can imagine this is so," Filippini said. He looked at Andrew. "For I have read that before you came to New York, you, too, were a wild man of the West."

"A wild man of the West?" Falcon repeated with a little chuckle.

"Yes, well, I'm quite civilized now," Andrew said, interrupting Falcon before he could say anything else.

"Tonight, I am glad to say that I will personally see to the preparation of your dinner," Filippini told them.

"Venendo alla nostra tavola lei c'onora, Signore Filippini," Andrew said.

"No, il mio amico. L'onore è ogni miniera perché Lei e Sua bella sorella scegliete di venire a Delmonicos," Filippini replied.

"What was that language?" Falcon asked after the chef left. "It wasn't Spanish."

"Chef Filippini is Italian," Andrew said. "I told him that, by his visit to our table, he honored us. He replied that we and our beautiful sister honored him by coming to Delmonico's."

"I'm impressed," Falcon said.

"Because I speak Italian?" Andrew chuckled. "There are one million people who live in New York, Falcon, and half of them are immigrants. Sometimes, just to walk through the streets of the city is like taking a world tour. You will hear dozens of languages being spoken."

The food was delivered then, and as they ate, Falcon answered questions about their mutual brothers, one of whom was sheriff of the county, and another of whom was mayor of the town of MacCallister.

After dinner, dessert was brought and this time Falcon, who had sat out the main course, joined them, eating a piece of chocolate cake with his coffee.

"This is good," Falcon said.

"Uh, Falcon," Andrew began. "About what I was saying to Filippini earlier . . . the wild man of the West thing."

"What about it?" Falcon asked.

"What you have to understand is that I must allow certain — illusions — to exist in order to enhance my persona."

"Enhance your persona? That's pretty highfalutin talk for a wild man of the West, isn't it?" Falcon teased. "Just exactly what illusions are you using to enhance your persona? It would help me to know that in order that I not step on your toes, so to speak."

"Well, I, uh, was a gunfighter in the Johnson County War," Andrew said. "And I had a showdown with Billy the Kid." Andrew sighed. "Also, I was standing by Wyatt Earp's side in the gunfight in Tombstone."

"They are calling that the Showdown at the OK Corral now," Falcon said. "You might want to refer to it that way."

"Thanks," Andrew said. "As you can see, I've pretty much taken all the things you've done — and told them as if I had done them."

"I'm flattered," Falcon said.

"You won't give him away, will you, Falcon?" Rosanna asked anxiously.

Smiling, Falcon made a clucking sound as he shook his head. "Andrew, Andrew, Andrew," he said. "No, of course I'm not going to give you away. But what I don't understand is why you would want to borrow anything from my life. I've been nothing but a drifter since Marie and our pa were killed. I've certainly done nothing as glamorous as all this."

Falcon took in the restaurant with a sweep

of his hand, but all knew that the gesture encompassed much more than just the restaurant.

"What have we done but speak a few lines, sing a few songs, and dance a little?" Andrew replied in a self-deprecating way.

"On the contrary," Falcon replied. "I was at the theater for the performance tonight. I watched how the audience reacted to the two of you. They love you."

Andrew and Rosanna looked across the table at each other, smiling at Falcon's words. It was easy, at this moment, to see that they were twins.

"It does have its satisfying moments," Andrew admitted.

Falcon took the last bite of his cake, then wiped his lips with a table linen before he spoke. "You were right, Rosanna, this is very good cake. I'm not sure I would die for it, but I would kill for it."

"What?" Rosanna gasped.

Falcon laughed. "I'm teasing."

"Perhaps," Rosanna said. "But with everything I've heard about you, one never knows when you are teasing and when you are serious."

"Oh? And what have you heard about me?" Falcon asked.

"I have heard that, while you have no fear,

95

your very name instills fear in others," Rosanna said.

Falcon looked at Andrew. "And that's the reputation you want for yourself?" he asked.

Andrew coughed nervously. "As I said, little brother, a degree of élan is absolutely de rigueur if one is to succeed on stage in New York."

"Tell, me, Falcon, what brings you to New York?" Rosanna asked. She held up her hand. "Don't get me wrong — as I said back in the theater, you are certainly welcome to come anytime you want. But you must admit this is not a place you visit often."

"I guess this is as good a time as any to bring it up," Falcon said. "I just didn't want to jump right into it."

"Jump right into what?" Andrew asked.

"Into the favor I'm going to ask of you."

Andrew and Rosanna looked at each other for a moment. "Falcon, if you need money, please don't hesitate to ask. You know that Rosanna and I will gladly give you . . ."

Falcon interrupted Andrew with a laugh and a raised hand.

"Andrew, have you forgotten that much about our family? Don't you know that Pa left us a fortune? And I've had some pretty successful ventures of my own, including a silver mine down in Arizona, a stagecoach line, and a very successful ranch. I have more money than I could spend in three lifetimes."

"Then, what is it? What kind of favor could Rosanna and I possibly do for you?"

"You do remember Colorado Springs, don't you?"

"Yes, of course we do," Rosanna said. "It's a place where people with consumption go to take the waters and the cures."

Falcon nodded. "Yes. My old friend Doc Holliday was there. But it's much more than a place where people come to take the cure now. It is also a place where people come to see the mountains, enjoy the West, and to stay in the Broadmoor."

"The Broadmoor?" Andrew said. He shook his head. "I don't remember the Broadmoor."

"No, you couldn't remember it because it wasn't there the last time you were in Colorado. How long has it been anyway?"

"How long has what been?"

"Since the two of you were in Colorado."

"Oh, heavens, I don't know. Six or seven years at least."

"You should come for a visit," Falcon said. "It will not be a hard trip. There is train service from New York all the way to Colorado Springs now. You'll have to change trains a few times, but that's not a problem."

"Yes, well, I would like to get back out there sometime," Rosanna said. "I would like to see our brothers, and to visit our parents' grave, and just have a look around at the place of my youth."

"Good, then it's all settled," Falcon said. "You'll come to Colorado Springs and you'll play at the Broadmoor."

"What? What do you mean it's all settled?" Andrew said. "And what do you mean we will play at the Broadmoor? That's the second time you have mentioned that. Just exactly what is the Broadmoor, anyway?"

"The Broadmoor is the best hotel west of the Mississippi River," Falcon said. "It is also a restaurant, nearly as good as this one, as well as a gambling establishment and a theater. When I say that you will play there, of course I mean that you will perform your act there." Falcon smiled. "Think about it. You'll win over thousands of new admirers."

"Why in heaven's name would I want to do something like that?" Andrew asked.

"Because I told James you would," Falcon replied.

"You told James? Who is James?"

"Count James Pourtales," Falcon said. "He has seen you perform, both here in

New York and in Europe. He is one of your biggest admirers, and when he learned I was your brother, it really lifted me in his eyes. I must say, it made me very proud to be able to claim you."

"No," Andrew said determinedly. "I will not go to some jerkwater town in the wilds of the West and perform like some court jester. It is a matter of artistic integrity."

"Andrew," Rosanna scolded. "What is wrong with you? Of course we will go. It sounds to me as if Falcon has given his word. Surely you haven't forgotten the lessons we learned from Papa, have you? He always told us, it is family above all other things."

"I remember. And I'm sorry that Falcon gave his word, I really am. But this family thing goes both ways. He should have checked with us before he did such a thing. Anyway, even if we did agree to go, can you see us convincing our manager? He gets ten percent of all our earnings. How are we going to explain to him that we are going to play at some hotel establishment in Colorado Springs in order to generate goodwill for our brother? What is ten percent of goodwill?"

"About twenty-five hundred dollars," Falcon said easily.

99

The expression on Andrew's face changed from one of anger to one of shock.

"I beg your pardon? Did you say twenty-five hundred dollars? What do you mean, twenty-five hundred dollars?"

"That would be your manager's percentage of goodwill."

Andrew shook his head. "I'm sure I have no idea what you are talking about."

"Unless my math is faulty, ten percent of twenty-five thousand dollars is twenty-five hundred dollars," Falcon explained.

"Twenty-five *thousand* dollars?" Andrew said, coming down hard on the word "thousand."

"That's the amount Count Pourtales has agreed to pay you if you will come for two weeks."

"Wait a minute," Andrew said, his interest clearly piqued now. "Are you saying he will pay us that much just for two weeks' work?"

"Yes."

"But that's impossible. We don't get that much in six months on the New York stage."

"I told you, the count is a very big admirer."

"A count?" Rosanna asked. "Is that just something people call him, or is he . . ."

"He is a real count," Falcon said, interrupting Rosanna's question.

"Two weeks, you say?" Andrew asked.

"Two weeks."

Andrew looked across the table at his sister. "What do you say, Rosanna? Should we take two weeks from our busy schedule to go to Colorado Springs for twenty-five thousand dollars?"

"I already told him I would go for nothing," Rosanna said. "With or without you, I would go. After all, he is our brother."

"That's true," Andrew said, more acquiescent now. "He is our brother, and what sort of siblings would we be if we did not answer his call for help?"

Sighing, Rosanna shook her head. "What sort of siblings indeed?" she asked quietly.

"Very well, Falcon, since you have given your word to the count, we will go," Andrew said.

"Thank you," Falcon said. He smiled. "It's good to see that your artistic integrity can be bought."

For just a moment Andrew flashed an expression of anger; then, suddenly, he broke out laughing.

"Touché, little brother. Touché."

CHAPTER EIGHT

As they were leaving the restaurant a few minutes later, a policeman came toward them and held up his hand.

"Aren't you the MacCallisters?" he asked Andrew.

"Yes," Andrew replied. "We'll be glad to sign an autograph, but you are going to have to furnish the paper and pen, I fear."

"No," the police officer said. "It's nothin' like that. I'm going to have to ask you to come with me."

"Come with you? Why?" Andrew asked, surprised by the officer's request.

"We've received a warning that your lives may be in danger. I'm to protect you."

"How do you plan to protect us?" Falcon asked.

"Who are you?" the policeman replied.

"This is my brother, Falcon," Andrew said.

"You can go your own way," the policeman said to Falcon. "My orders were to protect you and your sister," he added to Andrew, "not all three of you."

"Whatever you have in mind for us must include Falcon," Andrew insisted.

The policeman sighed. "Very well, but we must move quickly. I want you folks to come this way," he said, pointing toward the alley.

"You want us to go into that alley? What on earth for?" Andrew asked.

"It's police business," the policeman said, a bit more gruffly this time. "Don't give me any trouble now."

"It just seems odd that you would want us to go into an alley with you," Andrew said. "In all the time I've lived in New York, I've tried to avoid dark alleys, particularly at night."

"Into the alley with you now, and don't give me any more of your trouble!" the policeman said. This time his words were much gruffer than before, and he reached out to give Andrew a slight push.

"What is your badge number?" Falcon asked.

"My badge number? Why do you want to know my badge number? Are you going to report me for doing my job?" the policeman asked.

"No," Falcon said, stepping up to the officer. He put his hand over the shield. "I just want to know if you know your number."

"Of course I know it," the policeman replied. "It's . . ." He paused. "It's . . ." he started again, then glanced down toward his badge, only to see Falon's hand covering it.

"It's two, seven, one, five," Falcon said without moving his hand.

"All right, it's two, seven, one, five. What does that mean?"

"Here is a funny thing about this badge number," Falcon said. "When we arrived, we were greeted by a policeman who was wearing this very badge. In fact, he was also wearing this coat, because I remember seeing this repair." He pointed to a mended spot on the police tunic. "You are a fake," Falcon concluded.

"You're crazy," the policeman said.

"What did you do with the other officer?" Falcon asked.

Suddenly, the policeman made a grab for his pistol, but when his hand reached the holster, it was empty.

"What the hell?" he grunted in surprise.

"Are you looking for this?" Falcon asked, holding up the policeman's gun.

"How did you . . . ?" the policeman started to ask. Then, deciding his personal safety was more important than his curiosity, he turned and started running.

"Help me find him," Falcon said to his shocked brother and sister.

"Find him? Find who?" Rosanna asked.

"The real policeman. He has to be around here somewhere."

Falcon stepped into the same alley the fake cop had wanted them to enter.

"Falcon, be careful back there," Andrew called. "Maybe we should find another policeman."

"We may not have time to find another one," Falcon called back.

"This frightens me," Rosanna said quietly to Andrew. "I wish he would come out of there."

A moment later, they heard Falcon's voice calling from the darkness of the alley.

"I've found him, but he has been hurt. Stop a carriage; we need to get him to a doctor."

Two passing carriages failed to stop, and Falcon reappeared from the alley as a third was approaching. Like the other two carriages, it was a carriage for hire, and though the driver wasn't carrying a fare, he made no effort to stop.

Both Andrew and Rosanna waved at the driver.

"Stop, please, you must stop! It is an

emergency!" Andrew called.

Disregarding Andrew's emergency plea, the driver snapped his whip over the head of his team, urging them into an even quicker gait.

"He isn't going to stop," Rosanna said.

"Oh, he'll stop all right," Falcon said.

Suddenly, the night was lit up by the flash of gunfire, and the boom of the pistol came echoing back from all the surrounding buildings.

Rosanna screamed, then looked over toward Falcon to see that he was still holding the pistol he had taken from the fake cop. A little wisp of smoke was curling up from the barrel.

"Falcon, what . . . ?" she shouted. Then she saw that the carriage had come to a sudden stop as one of the horses had fallen to the pavement.

"You son of a bitch!" the driver yelled in anger. "You shot one of my horses!"

"Yes," Falcon said. "And I'm going to shoot you if you don't get that horse out of his traces and help us get this man to the hospital."

"I'll do nothing of the kind," the driver said. Jumping down from the carriage, he started toward Falcon, holding the whip over his hand. "What I'm going to do is leave lash marks on your face."

Falcon fired a second time, and this time his bullet cut the whip away from the handle.

The driver looked at the whip, then looked at Falcon, finally getting the message that Falcon wasn't a man to mess with.

Falcon aimed the pistol at the driver.

"Get that dead horse out of the traces and hook up the other one, then take us to a hospital," he said.

"Yes, sir, mister," the driver replied. "Yes, sir, whatever you say."

When they reached the hospital, Rosanna went inside and informed the attendants that they had an injured policeman. Two men with a stretcher came for the policeman, and as they started back inside, Andrew and Rosanna followed.

Falcon remained behind, and Andrew turned toward him. "Aren't you coming in?"

"I'll be there in a minute," Falcon said. He looked up at the driver, who was sitting in his seat, barely able to conceal his anger. "Thank you for bringing us," Falcon said.

"Well, now, it isn't like I had much of a choice, is it?" the driver replied.

"No, I guess you didn't."

"If I had known there was a man needed to get to the hospital, I would've took him.

You should'a told me."

"We did tell you."

"Yeah, by shootin' my horse."

"How much did you pay for that horse?"

"I paid one hundred dollars for him, mister. You cost me one hundred dollars tonight."

Falcon pulled out his billfold, then took out some money.

"Here's two hundred," he said. He nodded toward the single remaining horse. "I imagine he was so used to teaming with the other one that he might balk at teaming with a new horse. So you are going to have to get two new ones."

"What?" the driver asked in surprise. The glum expression left his face, to be replaced by a broad smile.

"Does this square us?" Falcon asked, holding out the money but not letting it go just yet.

The driver nodded. "Yes, sir, I reckon it more'n squares us."

Falcon stepped back from the carriage. "Get on with you, then," he said.

The driver slapped his reins against the back of the remaining horse, and the carriage pulled away from the curved drive in front of the hospital.

When Falcon went inside, he saw Andrew

and Rosanna sitting in chairs near the wall. He walked over to join them.

"One of the people said the doctor would come out to talk to us in a few minutes," Andrew said.

"All right," Falcon said, sitting in a chair beside them.

"Falcon, would you really have shot that driver?" Rosanna asked.

"Yes."

"Yes?"

"Someone told me a long time ago that you should never point a gun at someone unless you are willing to use it. I've never forgotten that lesson."

Rosanna shuddered. "Who in the world told you such a thing?"

"Our pa," Falcon said easily.

At that moment a small, gray-haired man came over toward them.

"Are any of you the MacCallisters?" the man asked.

"We all are," Rosanna answered for them.

"My goodness, the whole family must be here."

"Not quite the whole family," Falcon answered with a chuckle, thinking of their six other siblings and their children.

"Yes, well, I am Dr. Block. I just examined the patient. Is he your relative?"

"No, he is a policeman," Andrew said. "We found him injured and brought him here."

Dr. Block nodded. "Is that so? Well, he owes his life to the fact that you were all Good Samaritans."

"You mean he is going to be all right?" Rosanna asked.

"Yes, thanks to the fact that you got him here in time for us to treat him. I predict that he will be make a full recovery."

"Thank God," Rosanna said, breathing a sigh of relief.

CHAPTER NINE

Shortly after Andrew and Rosanna arrived, Count Pourtales took Rosanna on a tour of Broadmoor.

"I can see that a lot of planning went into this," she said.

"Yes, my dear," Pourtales replied. "I have been thinking about it for some time. My first thought was to concentrate on the families and friends who come with the invalids to the sanatoriums. You know that such visits have to be upsetting for them, with a loved one here who is in bad health. I wanted to give them something to do that would allow them to pass their time while they are here, as well as get their minds off their troubles. And this sort of diversion may well appeal to them. That is, those who like to gamble."

"But it looks to me as if you offer much more than gambling."

"Oh, indeed," Pourtales replied. "We have

a restaurant with a French chef, and a pavilion for dancing. And there is every kind of sport imaginable: boating, fishing, shooting, baseball, cricket matches. . . ."

"Cricket matches?" Rosanna asked with a little laugh.

"Yes. We have a lot of Londoners who visit, you know, so the cricket matches are for them. And, in time, we will have a golf course as fine as any they have in the East. Actually, what we are building here is something called a country club."

"A country club? I'm not sure I've ever heard the term before," Rosanna said.

"That's not surprising, even for someone as worldly as you," Pourtales said. "There is only one other in the United States."

"You consider me worldly, Count Pourtales?" Rosanna asked, lifting one eyebrow.

"Oh, my!" Pourtales said, clasping his hand to his mouth. "Please, my dear, take no offense. I meant nothing untoward about it. I just . . ."

Rosanna interrupted him with her laughter. "I know you didn't," she said. "I was just teasing you."

Pourtales clucked his tongue and shook his head. "I can see why you have so many admirers," he said. "You are not only beautiful and talented, you have a marvelous sense of humor. I do hope you enjoy your stay with us."

"I'm sure I will."

"And your brother?"

"I'm sure my brother will enjoy it as much as I."

At that moment, Falcon MacCallister was walking through the lobby of the Broadmoor. Seeing a pile of newspapers on the front desk, he left a nickel, picked up a paper, and walked out onto the front porch. He walked halfway down the length of the porch until he found a rocking chair that allowed him to enjoy the scenery, but was far enough away from passersby to enable him to read his paper in peace.

Some guests were playing croquet on the front lawn, and he heard a young woman's squeal of delight and a man's loud guffaw over a stroke. Unfolding the paper, he began to read and, as he had expected, the lead story was about the visit of his famous brother and sister.

AMUSEMENTS
AT BROADMOOR.

Famous New York Actors to Appear.

Brought to Colorado at Great Expense.

James Pourtales announced today that the famous thespians Andrew and Rosanna MacCallister have been contracted to present a show of song, dance, and dramatic readings in the theater at Broadmoor Casino.

Colorado Springs has in the past been woefully insufficient so far as entertainment and amusement for its visitors are concerned. To some, the natural scenes of canyons and mountains and pleasant drives afford all that is necessary in this line, but there are many others who seek their lost health in this most beneficent atmosphere who require other diversions than that provided so lavishly by nature, and who, if they cannot find it here, will seek it elsewhere. It is a well-authenticated fact that in many instances in the past people whose weakened hearts or leisurely habits prevented them from engaging in more serious occupations have left Colorado Springs for a residence in other places less beautiful, less bountifully endowed by nature, and less attractive in other ways, because they could not find that "something to do" which was lacking here.

The Broadmoor company has been the first to supply the want which many have recognized, and may fairly be said to mark an epoch in the history of the city. In bringing to our fair city acts of the quality of the MacCallisters, Count Pourtales is providing entertainment not only for the citizens who are already inhabitants of Colorado Springs, but also for a class who when they came here were not contented to remain.

Although the story of the MacCallisters' upcoming show at Broadmoor was the lead story of the *Colorado Springs Gazette,* there was another story, also on the front page, that caught Falcon's attention.

A SAVAGE MURDER!

Word has reached this newspaper of a tragic and savage event occurring within our own county. The bodies of Elam Rafferty and his wife, son, and daughter were found in their home last week. Mr. Rafferty and his son had both been shot in the head. Mrs. Rafferty and her daughter were stabbed to death. There is also evidence that both Mrs. Rafferty and her sixteen-year-old daughter had unspeakable horrors visited upon them before they were killed.

The bodies were found by Mr. Lamont Peabody. Mr. Peabody had made arrangements to buy six horses from Rafferty, and when Rafferty did not show on the day agreed upon, Peabody grew anxious. He gave Rafferty two more days, then rode out to the Rocking R Ranch to ascertain as to why Rafferty had not kept the appointment.

That was when he found all four bodies.

Peabody has been assured by Dr. Butler that an earlier arrival would not have enabled him to save the life of the young girl. Speculation as to the possibility arose when it was discovered that the young girl had lived long enough to inscribe, in blood, the name of her killer. The name was "Tate," and it is thought that she was referring to Loomis Tate, who avoided hanging in the week previous, by killing Deputy Leroy Coleman and making good his escape from the jail in Colorado Springs.

A note left at the jail was signed by both Loomis Tate and his brother Kelly. The note indicated that the Tates plan to take revenge on Mr. Falcon MacCallister for killing their brother Drew, during an attempted robbery of the stage between MacCallister and Colordao Springs.

Sheriff Smith visited the scene of the crime, then vowed a renewed effort to bring the nefarious Loomis Tate and his gang to a swift and unremitting justice.

After reading the newspaper, Falcon unfolded the note Sheriff Smith had given him when he returned from New York.

TO FALCON MACALESTER

WE ARE
^I AM GOING TO GIT EVIN WITH YOU FOR KILLIN MY BROTHER LIKE YOU DUN JUST YOU WAIT AND SEE.

LOOMIS TATE
KELLY TATE

Falcon didn't expect any trouble from Loomis Tate, who, he was sure, was far from Colorado Springs by now, but he had learned long ago to always be on the alert.

A shadow passed over him and, looking up, he saw his sister.

"So, here you are," Rosanna said. "Enjoying the air, are you?"

"Yes, very much," Falcon replied. He pointed to the paper. "And the story about you and Andrew. The editor gave the two of

117

you quite a write-up."

"Yes, I saw it. It was almost embarrassingly flattering," Rosanna said. "Count Pourtales has just given me a grand tour of the facilities."

"It's quite a place, isn't it?"

"Yes, it's very lovely. And our rooms. They are nicer than any hotel room I have ever visited."

Falcon, Andrew, and Rosanna had each been given luxurious rooms in the rear of the hotel.

"Have you seen the view from our balcony?" Rosanna asked.

"Yes."

"It is breathtakingly beautiful," she said. Spontaneously, she leaned down and hugged her brother. "Oh, Falcon, I can't thank you enough for setting all this up for us."

"I was just the messenger," Falcon said.

"Whatever your part in it, I thank you."

"Rosanna, oh, there you are!" Andrew called from down the porch. "I've been looking everywhere for you."

"Well, I've been everywhere," Rosanna joked. "The wonder is that we didn't cross paths."

"There is no time for joking now," Andrew said. "Come on, we need to get dressed for the first number."

"I'll be right there," Rosanna promised. She smiled at Falcon. "Where will you be sitting? I always like to play to someone special, and tonight that will be you. But I can't do it if I don't know where you will be sitting."

"I'm not sure yet," Falcon replied.

Andrew walked up just as Falcon was answering Rosanna's question.

"Of course you know where you'll be sitting," Andrew said. "You'll be in Count Pourtales's box."

"He's not a count over here," Falcon said.

"My dear boy, you simply don't understand," Andrew said. "Once a count, always a count. Come along, my dear," he said to Rosanna. "We simply must get into our first costume."

Falcon watched them walk away. Then he smiled and shook his head.

"Papa," he said. "How in the hell did those two wind up in Mama's litter?"

CHAPTER TEN

As fiddles, flutes, and drums played behind them, Andrew and Rosanna performed an Irish step dance, their feet tapping rapidly on the stage floor while they were practically motionless from their waists up.

After the dance, Rosanna left the stage, then returned to bring a hat and cane to Andrew. Andrew put the hat on his head, tipped it forward, leaned upon the cane like a dandy, and began his song.

I came home the other night,
As drunk as I could be.
And what do you think my wondering
   eyes should see?
A horse, where my horse should be.
So I said to my wife, my pretty little wife,
"Explain this thing to me.
What's a horse doing where my horse
   should be?"
And she said, "You old fool, you drunken

old fool,
Can't you plainly see?
That's nothing but a milk cow
My mama gave to me."

The audience roared with appreciative laughter and Andrew went on:

Well, I've been around this country,
Maybe ten times or more,
But a saddle and a bridle on a milk cow
I never saw before.

More laugher.

I came home the other night,
As drunk as I could be,
And what do you think my wondering
    eyes should see?

"What did you see?" someone yelled from the crowd.
Playing to the crowd, Andrew lifted a finger, then shook his head as if confused by the whole thing.

I saw a hat, hanging on the hat rack,
Where my hat ought to be.
So I said to my wife, my pretty little wife,
"Explain this thing to me.
What's this hat doing on the hat rack,

Where my hat ought to be?"
And she said, "You old fool, you drunken
   fool,
Can't you plainly see?
That's nothing but a chamber pot
My mama gave to me."
Well, I've been around this country,
Maybe ten times or more.
But a feather on a chamber pot
I never saw before.

There was more laughter.

"Come on, mister, you didn't believe that, did you?" someone yelled.

"What happened next?" another from the audience called.

Andrew, playing the injured and innocent husband, tipped his hat back, stepped forward as if taking the audience into his confidence, and continued.

I came home the other night,
As drunk as I could be.
And what do you think my wondering
   eyes should see?

"Mister, the way it's been going with you, there's no tellin' what you seen!" someone yelled, and again, the crowd roared with laughter. Andrew, playing the crowd beautifully, merely raised one eyebrow as if totally taken in by it all, then continued.

I saw my pants, on a chair,
Where my pants ought to be.

"Mister, you had better wake up," one of the men in the audience shouted.

So I said to my wife, my pretty little wife,
"Explain this thing to me.
What are these pants doing here,
Where my pants ought to be?"

"Ha! I'd like to hear how she got out of that one!" someone said.

And she said, "You old fool, you drunken
    fool,
Can't you plainly see?
That's nothing but a dishrag
My mama sent to me."
Now, I've been around this country,
Maybe ten times or more.
But belt and buttons on a dishrag
I never saw before.

"Why, you old fool! Don't you know what she's doing to you?" someone in the front row yelled.

I came home the other night
As drunk as I could be.
And what do you think my wondering
   eyes should see?
A head, on the pillow,
Where my head should be.

"I told you!" one of the men in the audience shouted. "You should've figured it out
the moment you saw that strange horse."
  Andrew raised his hand and pointed his
finger. He made a face like an irate husband,
challenging his wife with irrefutable evidence.

So I said to my wife, my pretty little wife,
"Explain this thing to me.
What is this head doing on my pillow,
Where my head should be?"
And she said, "You old fool, you drunken
   fool,
Can't you plainly see?
That's nothing but a mushmelon
My mama sent to me."

"A mushmelon?" one of the audience
yelled. "She said it was a mushmelon and
you believed her?"

Well, I've been around this country,
Maybe ten times or more.

But a mustache on a mushmelon
I never saw before.
Yes, a mustache on a mushmelon
I never saw before.

Andrew finished his song with a sweeping
bow, and then left the stage to the howls of
laughter from an appreciative audience.

When Andrew was finished, Rosanna
returned to the stage. She had changed
costumes, and was now wearing a beautiful
green dress that showed off her hair, skin,
and exquisite shape to perfection. She was
holding a single yellow rose as she began to
sing:

Over in Killarney
Many years ago,
Me Mither sang a song to me
In tones so sweet and low.
Just a simple little ditty,
In her good ould Irish way,
And I'd give the world if she could sing
That song to me this day.
Too-ra-loo-ra-loo-ral, too-ra-loo-ra-li,
Too-ra-loo-ra-loo-ral, hush now, don't you
   cry!
Too-ra-loo-ra-loo-ral, too-ra-loo-ra-li,
Too-ra-loo-ra-loo-ral, that's an Irish lullaby.

The audience, which had been roaring

with laughter over Andrew's ditty, now wiped tears from their eyes at the purity and sweetness of Rosanna's voice.

The best form of advertisement is word of mouth, and word of the MacCallisters' performance spread throughout Colorado and even into the adjacent states. Extra trains were put on, and Pourtales had to bring in extra chairs to accommodate the increased audience. Andrew and Rosanna finished their last night's performance to a crowd that was standing room only. After that, they were invited to a dinner given by Count Pourtales to honor Andrew and Rosanna. The members of the band and the stage crew had also been invited.

Falcon was invited as well, and he sat at the head table with Pourtales and his brother and sister.

"My friends," Pourtales said from the head table to all the guests in the room. He lifted his glass. "I drink a toast to the most talented two performers in the world: to Andrew and Rosanna MacCallister."

"Hear, hear," someone else said, and they all lifted their wineglasses and drank.

Andrew stood to speak.

"Ladies and gentlemen of this wonderful city of Colorado Springs, I must confess that when my brother approached us to come here, I was somewhat reticent. After all, my sister and I had trod the boards of the New York stage and played the theaters of Europe. What could there possibly be for us here?

"Well, I was wrong. I was very wrong. Never have we appeared in a more beautiful setting; never have we been better received than by the marvelous audiences who applauded our meager effort. To the talented and skilled cast and production staff who served us, and to Count James Pourtales, our most gracious host who made all possible, my sister and I give you our heartfelt thanks."

City Gives MacCallisters A Gala Send-Off

The day broke fair and beautiful this morning, seeming to smile upon the occasion. At an early hour the streets began to fill with people and there was the sound of music and marching feet. Many of the merchants decorated their stores with flags and bunting in honor of the two noted thespians who, for the two weeks previous, have so gallantly graced our city by their presence.

The parade started promptly at nine o'clock, forming opposite the city hall on Nevada Avenue. First came a platoon of volunteer firemen, all attired in uniform and presenting their usual fine and commanding appearance. Then came the sheriff and all his deputies, mounted upon spirited horses. Following came the Centennial State band with fourteen pieces discoursing martial strains par excellence led by Drum Major M. O. Barns, the band fully sustaining its well-merited standing as one of the best in the West. Next came the school cadets with twenty-one men in line and with their neat and attractive uniforms and their glistening rifles attracting more than usual attention. They were followed by a marching element of the Knights of Pythias, then the Pikes Peak lodge of I.O.O.F. That was followed by a rifle and drum corps of the Grand Army of the Republic. Next came Mayor Sprague and members of the city council, after which came the children of the city schools, many of them carrying wreaths and bouquets of wildflowers in the full glee and merriment of childhood, presenting one of the most pleasing features of the procession. Their participation will doubtless ensure that, even into the next century, stories will be told of this festive event, for it shall long be remembered by them.

And, finally, as the last unit of the parade, came the subjects of the city's adoration. The world-famous actors, Andrew and Rosanna MacCallister, were riding with James Pourtales in his shining green and gold carriage, driven by a liveried coachman and attended by two elegantly uniformed footmen.

The parade ended at the depot, where the entire town sent the two off with song and glad tidings.

CHAPTER ELEVEN

Although he wasn't sure how far they had come, Loomis Tate believed that they were at least two hundred miles east of Colorado Springs.

For several minutes now, they had been approaching a small town. It had risen before them almost as if it were a natural part of the terrain, the buildings blending into the prairie with both their irregular shape and indistinct color.

At the edge of town they saw a building, a rambling, unpainted wooden structure that stretched and leaned and bulged and sagged until it looked as if the slightest puff of wind might blow it down. A sign out front read:

ZIEGENHORN'S
Groceries – Eats – Rooms

Loomis started heading toward the building.

"Hey, Loomis, what are you goin' in there for? Let's go on into town and find us a real saloon," Strayhorn said.

"Yeah," the albino agreed. "I'm so thirsty I could spit dust."

"We need some supplies," Loomis said. "We'll get 'em here, then go find a saloon."

"What we could use is some more money," Kelly said. "I think we should rob the place."

"No," Loomis said. "Not here. Not yet."

"Well, tell me, Loomis, just how much longer do you expect we can get by on what little money we got?"

"We'll get some more money," Loomis said. "We just ain't goin' to get it here, is all."

The men tied off their horses out front, then stepped onto the porch. A nondescript yellow dog was sleeping in the shade of the porch, so secure with his position and the surroundings that he didn't even open his eyes as they went around him to go inside.

The interior of Ziegenhorn's was a study of shadow and light. Some of the light came through the door, and some came through windows that were nearly opaque with dirt. Most of it, however, was in the form of gleaming dust motes that hung suspended in the still air, illuminated by the bars of

131

sunbeams that stabbed through the cracks between the boards.

There were three men sitting around a cracker barrel at the back of the room. One of them, wearing an apron, was obviously the proprietor. But one of them, Loomis noticed with some alarm, was wearing a badge.

"Howdy," the proprietor said affably. "What can I get for you gents?"

"Your sign out front says you have groceries," Loomis said.

"Yes, sir, we got groceries, we got dry goods, just about anything you might need, you can get it right here."

"How about whiskey?" the albino said.

"No, sir, town ordinance says you can't serve liquor unless you got a license, and since the marshal is right here keepin' an eye on me, well, I reckon I better not do that," the proprietor said with a chuckle. "But you might try the Long Trail, it's . . ." It wasn't until that moment that the proprietor actually noticed the albino, and so startled was he by the pasty white appearance that he stopped in mid-sentence.

"Something wrong, mister?" the albino asked.

The proprietor shook his head. "No," he said. "No, sir, nothing at all is wrong. Uh, you said you wanted some supplies."

"For travelin'," Loomis said.

"Where you boys from?" the man with the badge asked.

"We're up from the South," Loomis said.

At the same time Loomis was saying "South," Kelly said "West."

The lawman looked confused. "Well, which is it? South or West?"

"Both," Loomis said.

"Both?"

"We're from Arizona. That's south and west of here."

The lawman chuckled and nodded. "Yeah," he said. "I can see where the confusion might come in. Well, you boys are certainly a long way from home. Where you headed?"

"That depends on where we are," Loomis said.

"What?"

"What's the name of this place?"

"Eagle Tail," the lawman replied. "It's not much of a place now, but we're on the railroad so I expect we'll be growin' somewhat. My name is Crack Kingsley, the fella that owns this place is Hank Ziegenhorn, and this is Tom Blanton. Blanton here is the editor of the paper," he added, indicating the man who was sitting on one of the other

133

chairs around the table.

"You the sheriff?"

Kingsley chuckled. "Hardly. I'm the city marshal is all. I didn't catch your names," Kingsley said.

"We ain't nobody important," Loomis answered. Then, to Blanton, in order to change the subject away from their names, he said, "Newspaper editor, huh? Well, shouldn't you be out gathering news or something?"

"No better place to gather news than right here," Blanton replied. "Lots of folks come in here right off the train. Sometimes I get news just by talking to them; other times I get news from the newspapers they leave behind."

It now seemed obvious that the lawman had not recognized them, and Loomis was not really interested in the conversation, but he let the editor continue.

"Yes, sir," Blanton continued. "Before I came here and started publishing the *Pronouncement,* I worked as a reporter for the *St. Louis Republican.* And now I use their stories, like the piece I did today about the MacCallisters."

"Your piece about who?" Loomis asked, suddenly showing more interest in the conversation. "Did you say MacCallisters?"

"Yes, sir, it's in the paper today," Blanton said. "The great thespians Andrew and Rosanna MacCallister came all the way out to Colorado Springs just to put on a show."

"Oh," Loomis replied, his interest waning again.

"Can you imagine that?" Blanton asked. "Why, the MacCallisters have played on the stage in New York, London, Paris — just about all over the world, I reckon, and they came all the way out here to put on a show for Westerners."

Loomis didn't reply and the newspaper editor, anxious to continue the conversation, spoke again.

"I know some folks are wondering why they did it, but it's not hard to figure out when you know the history of their family. I mean, their father was the famous James Ian MacCallister, and some say their brother Falcon is just as famous."

Once again, Loomis was interested.

"Did you say their brother is Falcon Mac-Callister?" he asked.

"Yes indeed. Heard of him, have you?"

"Yes, I've heard of him," Loomis said.

"Well, I don't doubt it. After all, they say that Falcon MacCallister is the most feared gunman in the West. And yet, or so it is told, he never uses his gun for evil, only for good and justice. You say you have heard of him. Do you know Falcon MacCallister, sir?"

"I've met him," Loomis said.

"What is he like? I'm told he is a prince of a fellow."

"That's him, all right," Loomis said. "None better."

Loomis could feel the eyes of the others on him, but no one said anything.

"Perhaps you would like to meet his brother and sister," Blanton suggested.

"Thanks," Loomis said. "But we're not headed for Colorado Springs."

"You misunderstand me, sir. You wouldn't have to go to Colorado Springs," Blanton said. "They're coming here."

"Here?" Loomis said. "Wait a minute, you're tellin' me how famous they are, how they've played all over the world, but they're going to come here and do a show?"

Blanton, Kingsley, and Ziegenhorn all laughed.

"Heavens, no," Ziegenhorn said. "They won't do a show here. Of course, I would love it if we could get them to sing just one song for us, but I don't think they will do that either. But they are going back to New York and their train will be passing through here tomorrow afternoon. And there is a chance that they might come out just long enough to wave at us."

"What makes you think they'd do that?" the albino asked. "I mean, for a little town like this?"

"Well, for all that they are rich and famous, I am told that they are very nice people," Blanton replied. "And I believe we can prevail upon them to at least say hello."

"We've made a sign," the proprietor said.

"What sort of a sign?"

"It's down at the depot. When you leave here, you should ride by and take a look at it."

"Maybe we'll just do that," Loomis said.

"Oh, and if you're planning on staying overnight so as to be here when they come through tomorrow, I've got some beds in the back," the proprietor said. "Maybe you seen my sign out front."

"Didn't notice," Loomis replied.

"Yes, sir, ten cents for a bed and a nickel for a blanket."

"We ain't got that much money," Loomis said. "I see no need in wastin' it on rooms, when we can sleep outside. But I will be takin' them supplies now, if you don't mind."

"Yes, sir," Ziegenhorn said. "I'll be glad to do that. What do you need?"

"Coffee, flour, bacon, beans, and salt,

enough to last the five of us for two weeks."

"Will that be all?"

"Yeah, that'll be all."

"Hey, Loomis, would you look here at this? Someone has actually written a book about the son of a bitch," Strayhorn said. He was looking at a display of books, and he picked up a penny dreadful to show to Loomis.

FALCON MacCALLISTER'S GREAT TRIUMPH

A Story of the Wild West

By
Jack Coulter

"Oh, are you a reader, sir?" Ziegenhorn asked, pointing to the book. "I have several books about Falcon MacCallister. Being as he is a friend of yours, you might particularly enjoy this one."

"I'm not much of a reader," Loomis said. He turned to Strayhorn. "Put the book down and let's go."

"He called MacCallister a son of a bitch," Ziegenhorn said after the five men left. "That doesn't sound like much of a friend to me, does it to you?"

"No, I can't say that it does," Blanton said.

"Hank," Kingsley said. "The fella that picked up the book, did he call the other Loomis?"

Ziegenhorn paused for a moment and stroked his chin.

"Yeah, I believe he did," Ziegenhorn said. "Loomis, Doomis, something like that. Why? Have you ever heard of him?"

"I'm not sure," Kingsley said. "But there's somethin' about the name that sort of sticks in my craw."

"Maybe you seen him on one of your wanted posters," Ziegenhorn suggested.

"Could be," Kingsley replied. "I'll take a look when I get back to the office.

As Loomis and the others rode by the depot, they saw a big sign stretched out in front of the building.

EAGLE TAIL WELCOMES
ANDREW AND ROSANNA
MacCALLISTER

"That's somethin', them bein' MacCallister's kin, ain't it?" Strayhorn asked.

"Yeah," Loomis replied. "Come on, let's go have that drink you fellas been belly-achin' about."

The Long Trail smelled of whiskey, stale beer, and sour tobacco. There was a long, polished mahogany bar on the left, with towels hanging on hooks about every five feet along its front. A large gilt-edged mirror was behind the bar.

Over against the back wall, near the foot of the stairs, a piano player sat at the handsome upright piano furnishing background music. There was a bowl on the piano for tips.

Out on the floor of the saloon, nearly all the tables were filled. A half-dozen or so bar gals were flitting about, pushing drinks and promising more than they really intended to deliver. A few card games were in progress, but most of the patrons were just drinking and talking. The subject of their conversation was the upcoming visit by the MacCallisters.

"I don't know what ever'one is so excited about," one of the patrons was saying. "It ain't like they're goin' to stop here and put on a show or nothin'."

"No, it ain't. But it would be somethin' just to see 'em. I mean they're about as famous as you can get," another said.

"Hell, their brother's just as famous."

"Out here maybe, but not back East. And

not in Europe. No, sir, I for one intend to be down to the train station to see 'em when they come through."

Loomis and the others bought a beer apiece, then found an empty table. One of the bar girls came over to the table.

"Hi, boys," she said, smiling. "My, what a handsome bunch of . . ." Seeing the albino, she stopped in midsentence, but bravely held her smile. ". . . cowboys you are," she said, completing her sentence. "Do you want some company?"

"Why, yeah," Strayhorn said. "Come on over and join us."

"Go away," Loomis said.

"Loomis, come on, we're . . ." Strayhorn began, but Loomis glared at him.

"Go away," he said again, and pouting, the girl retreated.

"What did you do that for?" Logan asked. "One of the reasons you come to drink in a saloon is because of the women."

"You can have women later," Loomis said. "Fact is, with the idea I got, you'll have enough money to have all the women you want."

"Idea? What kind of idea?"

"I know how I can get even with MacCallister, and make a lot of money besides."

"Really? How are you goin' to do that?"

141

Loomis didn't answer Strayhorn directly. Instead, he turned to his brother.

"Kelly, when's the last time you was in these parts?"

"Not more'n six months ago," Kelly answered.

"There used to be a stagecoach way station up at Gopher Creek. You reckon it's still there?" Loomis asked.

"Yeah, I suppose it is," Kelly replied. "But since the railroad come through, they don't use it anymore. There's nobody there."

"Good," Loomis said. "We can hole up there."

"Yeah, that might not be a bad idea," Kelly said. "How long do you plan to hole up?"

"For as long as it takes."

"As long as it takes for what?"

"For as long as it takes to get the money," Loomis said with no further explanation.

"I need me another drink," Strayhorn said.

"We ain't got enough money to waste on another drink, and we ain't got the time," Loomis said. "We need to get goin'."

"Get goin'? Get goin' where?"

"You want in on this or not?" Loomis asked.

"Well, yeah, I want in on it."

"Then just do as I say without belly-achin'." Loomis stood. "Come on, let's go."

CHAPTER TWELVE

They were about five miles out of town when Loomis stopped and pointed to two horses that were tied to a cottonwood tree.

"Let's go get them two horses," Loomis said. "We're goin' to be needin' 'em."

"What for?" Kelly asked.

"For my plan."

"You ain't told nobody what your plan is yet," Kelly said.

"I'll tell you when it comes time to tell you," Loomis said. "For now, we need them horses."

Loomis and the others rode up quietly to the two horses. Then they stopped and looked around. "You see anybody?" Loomis asked.

"No."

They heard the sound of laughter from just over a hill. The laughter sounded young.

"You give me my clothes back, Johnny, or I'll tell Mama!" a boy's voice said.

"Jesse is a baby, Jesse is a baby, run to Mama, Jesse."

The taunting voice was also that of a young boy.

"Take the horses," Loomis said, and Logan got down to untie them. Just as he did so, a young boy appeared at the top of the hill. His hair was wet and it was obvious he had been swimming. He was carrying a pair of britches and a shirt with him.

"You want your clothes, Jesse, come get them!" Johnny shouted back down the hill. Then, laughing, he turned and saw Loomis and the others taking the horses. The laughter left his face.

"Hey, mister! Get away from them horses! They belong to us!"

Throwing down the clothes, Johnny started running toward Logan.

"Brave little shit, ain't he?" Kelly said with a chuckle as they all watched him running toward Logan.

Suddenly, they were startled by the sound of a gunshot, and they saw a little spray of blood come from the hole in the middle of Johnny's forehead. He fell back.

Looking toward Loomis, they saw him holding a smoking pistol.

"Damn!" Logan said.

"Johnny! Johnny, what's going on?" another voice shouted.

Another boy, much younger than Johnny, appeared at the top of the hill. He too was wet from swimming, and because he was naked, it was obvious he had been skinny-dipping. When he saw Johnny, he cried out and ran to him.

"What the hell did you shoot that boy for?" Logan asked.

"Because he seen us," Loomis answered. "And we don't need anyone in these parts knowing who we are or what we look like."

Loomis turned and lowered his gun to shoot Jesse, but he wasn't there.

"What the hell?" Loomis said. "Where did he go?"

"I don't know, I don't see him," Kelly said.

"Look for him. We have to find him," Loomis said. "What did the boy call him? Jesse?"

"Yeah."

"Jesse!" Loomis called. "Jesse, come on out, we ain't goin' to shoot you! I'm sorry 'bout shootin' Johnny, but he run toward us and I thought he had a gun."

"You knew he didn't have no gun," Jesse called back.

Loomis started toward the sound of the voice. "I didn't mean to shoot him, and I won't shoot you. We just need to borrow a couple of horses, is all."

146

■ ■ ■ ■

Quietly Jesse slipped down into the water. Then, he lay on the bottom of the pond, breathing through a reed, the reed lost in a sea of reeds. It was a game he and Johnny often played, but this time it was for real.

Looking up through the shimmering surface of the water, he could see that a rider had come right down to the edge of the pond.

"Where are you, Jesse? I'll pay you for the horses."

"Loomis, there's someone comin' up the road," the albino called.

"Damn! All right, let's get out of here," Loomis said.

Jesse watched the rider turn and leave, but he knew better than to show himself yet. He made himself stay on the bottom for almost half an hour, longer than he had ever stayed underwater before.

Finally, Jesse got out of the pond and crawled up the side of the hill. Looking over toward the road, he saw that the riders were gone. Not until then did he put on his clothes. He didn't go back to look at Johnny. He knew that his brother was dead, and he didn't want to see him that way.

■ ■ ■ ■

Later that same night, Loomis, Logan, Strayhorn, the albino, and Kelly were waiting near a water tank alongside the Union Pacific track, some fifty miles east of Eagle Tail. It was nearly eleven p.m. and the rails, reflecting the full moon, formed parallel streaks of softly gleaming silver to stretch off into the distance.

One of the horses whickered, and another stomped its foot.

"Keep an eye on them horses, Michaels," Loomis said. "If they get away out here, we'll be left suckin' hind tit, and that's for sure."

"They ain't goin' nowhere," Michaels replied. "It's them two we just picked up that's a little nervous, but I'm keepin' a tight hold of 'em."

"Kelly, go up and see if you can see anything," Loomis ordered.

Kelly walked up to the track and stared back toward the west.

"You see anything?" Loomis asked. "A light or anything?"

"No, not a thing," Kelly answered. He got down on his knees, then leaned forward, putting his ear to the rail.

148

"What are you doin'?" Strayhorn asked.

"Sometimes you can hear a train comin' through the rails 'fore you can see it," Kelly explained.

"Well, do you hear anything?"

Kelly stood up, brushed off his knees, then his hands, and shook his head.

"No, I didn't hear nothin'."

"Are you sure the train will come this way?" Logan asked.

"No, it's prob'ly goin' to take a dirt road," Strayhorn said, and the others laughed.

"You know what I mean," Logan said. "I mean, what if it took another track?"

"There ain't no other track," Loomis said. "This here is the main line. It will come here." He pointed to the water tower. "And it will stop here to take on water."

"Hey, Loomis, how much money do you think we can get?" the albino asked.

"Well, the MacCallisters is rich people," Loomis said. "And I don't mean just the actors. I mean the whole damn family is rich. Especially Falcon MacCallister. He owns a silver mine down in Arizona, he has a big ranch, and him and his brothers own MacCallister Stage Lines. I expect they'll pay a lot to get their famous brother and sister back."

"Strayhorn, what you goin' to do with the

money when you get it?" Logan asked.

"I'm goin' to go back East someplace, like maybe St. Louis or Chicago, and buy me some new duds," Strayhorn answered. "Then, after that, I'm going to get me a cold piece of pie and a hot piece of ass."

On board the St. Louis Flyer, Andrew and Rosanna sat in facing seats in the Pullman car.

"This time next week we'll be back in New York," Andrew said.

"Yes," Rosanna answered.

Andrew chuckled. "That was a rather pensive yes, wasn't it?"

"Was it? I'm sorry, I guess my mind is somewhere else right now."

"You're thinking about our next show, aren't you? I understand Clinton Stuart is writing a new play called *Our Society.* I think it may have parts for us."

"Yes, I suppose so."

Andrew was puzzled by Rosanna's less than enthusiastic answer, and he cocked his head and stared at her for a moment.

"What's wrong?" he asked.

"Wrong? Nothing is wrong."

"Something is. You aren't yourself to-night."

Rosanna sighed. "Andrew, have you ever

thought about coming back?"

"Coming back? Coming back where?"

"Coming back here, back home," Rosanna said.

"Rosanna, I can't believe I'm hearing you talk like this," he said. "Ever since we were children, practically from the first time we could talk, we have wanted to be performers."

"That's true."

"And we have done that, Rosanna. We have lived a life that others can only dream of. We performed in the White House for President Rutherford B. Hayes; we were received by Queen Victoria herself. Surely you haven't forgotten that."

"Of course not," Rosanna replied. "No one can ever forget something like that."

"But now, you are saying you want to give it all up?"

Rosanna shook her head. "No, I didn't say that. I just asked if you ever thought about coming back home — someday."

"Someday? Sure, someday," Andrew said. "What got you started on this?"

"I don't know. It's just that, well, everyone was so wonderful to us, and there was such a freshness about it. I guess I was just getting very nostalgic, is all."

Andrew laughed softly. "Next thing I

know, you'll break out singing 'I'll Take You Home Again, Kathleen.' "

Rosanna laughed as well. "Touché," she said.

The porter stopped and touched the brim of his hat as he made a slight bow.

"Would the lady and gentleman like their beds made?"

"I think so," Rosanna said. "It has been a long day." She looked over at Andrew. "I'll take the top bunk," she said. "That way, if you aren't ready to go to bed yet, you won't have to."

"No, I'm ready as well," Andrew said. "You're right, it has been a long day."

The porter made the two beds quickly and expertly, then set the ladder so Rosanna could climb up to the upper bunk. She and Andrew exchanged good nights; then she lay in her bunk, listening to the rhythm of the wheels on the rails and rocking gently with the train's motion until she fell asleep.

"Loomis," Kelly called down from the track. "The train's a'comin', I can see the head-lamp."

"All right," Loomis said. "Michaels, you stay with the horses. The rest of you, come with me."

Loomis led the others to a stand of scrub

willow that grew alongside the track. This would provide them with concealment from the train as it arrived, but keep them close enough to act quickly.

The train was approaching at about twenty miles per hour, a respectable enough speed, though the vastness of the prairie made it appear as if the train was going much slower. From this distance, the train seemed small, and even the white smoke that poured from its stack made but a tiny iridescent scar against the starry vault of midnight sky.

They could hear the train quite easily, the sound of its puffing engine carrying across the wide, flat ground.

"What if the train don't stop?" Logan asked.

"It has got to take on water," Loomis said. "It'll stop."

"Well, look at it, it ain't a'slowin' down none," Logan said.

Almost as soon as Logan said the words, they heard the steam valve close and the train began to brake. As the engine approached, it gave some perspective as to how large the prairie really was, for the train that had appeared so tiny before was now a behemoth, blocking out the sky. It ground to a reluctant halt, its stack puffing smoke, and its driver wheels wreathed in tendrils of white steam that seemed to glow as it drifted away in the darkness.

"All right, wait until the fireman starts putting the water in," Loomis ordered. "They'll be payin' so much attention to that, they won't notice us."

"We're goin' to get us some money too, right, Loomis?" Strayhorn asked.

"Don't worry, when MacCallister gets wind that we've got his brother and sister, he'll come up with the money."

"I mean some money for right now," Strayhorn said.

"Yeah, I've already got that taken care of," Loomis said. He showed Strayhorn a cloth bag. "We're goin' to take up a little collection. Folks that can afford to travel in a Pullman car will, like as not, have a lot of money with 'em."

"What about the other cars?" Strayhorn asked. "Don't you think we ought to go through all them as well?"

"No, we won't have time for that," Loomis said. "We're here to get the MacCallisters, and that's what we're goin' to do. We'll rob the folks that's in the Pullman, take the MacCallisters, and be on our way."

"What about the express car?" Strayhorn asked.

"Look, Strayhorn, if you don't like ridin'

154

with me, go somewhere else."

"No, no," Strayhorn said, putting up his hands. "You're the boss."

"Try remembering that," Loomis said.

CHAPTER THIRTEEN

When the St. Louis Flyer made a midnight stop for water, Rosanna, who was asleep in the top berth of the Pullman car, was only vaguely aware that the stop had been made. She was too comfortable and too tired from all the hoopla of the last two weeks to give it too much attention.

Rolling over in bed, she pulled the covers up and listened to the conversation between the engineer and the fireman as they prepared to take on water.

"How's that, Austin? Am I lined up?" the engineer called back to the fireman.

"Yeah, Doodle, that's just fine," Austin answered.

The water started drumming into the tender.

"Hey, Doodle, do you have a valve open somewhere?" Austin called.

"No, why?"

"We must have a leak. The tank's damn

near empty. It shouldn't be this far down."

"We'll have it looked at when we get to St. Louis," Doodle said.

"Yeah, if we make it that far. Don't forget the run between Hays City and Russellville has a sixty-mile stretch between water tanks."

"Yeah, I know what you mean. I'll slow down through there; we'll use less water that way."

Although Rosanna could hear them talking quite clearly, it seemed as if they were very far away, and she felt herself drifting back to sleep.

Just outside the stopped train, Loomis, Kelly, Logan, and Strayhorn were waiting.

"All right, get your hoods on!" Loomis hissed.

The four men pulled hoods from their pockets and put them on. Then, with Loomis in the lead, the four men moved quickly alongside the railroad track, ducking occasionally so as not to throw any shadows onto the yellow squares that were projected onto the ground from the few windows that were showing light.

The train was alive with sound; from the loud puffs of the driver relief valves venting steam, to the splash of water filling the tank, to the snapping and popping of overheated bearings and gearboxes.

"Which car do you think they are they on?" Kelly asked.

"Well, they's only one Pullman car," Loomis said. "So that's the one they have to be on."

"All right, we know which car, but how are we goin' to find 'em?" Logan asked.

"We'll find them," Loomis answered. "Shhh," he said and, holding his hand out, signaled for everyone to get closer to the train. Then, looking toward the tender, he saw that the fireman had his back to them as he was directing the gushing water from the spout into the tank.

Loomis held out his hand. "All right, he ain't lookin' this way," he hissed. "Get up onto the vestibule."

Loomis waited until the other three had climbed onto the vestibule; then he climbed up behind them.

"Inside, let's go," he hissed.

Loomis pushed the door open and the four men stepped inside. The car was dimly lit by two low-burning gimbal-mounted lanterns, one on the front wall and the other on the rear. They walked down an aisle that was flanked by two rows of closed curtains, listening to the heavy breathing and snores of the passengers.

"Which berth you think they're in?" Logan asked.

"It don't matter which one they're in," Loomis replied.

"What do you mean it don't matter?"

"This is what I mean," Loomis said. Reaching up, he jerked the curtain open to the berth nearest him, then reached in and grabbed the hair of a young woman.

The woman screamed, but Loomis stopped the screaming by putting his hand over her mouth.

The scream had the effect, though, of waking everyone up and causing them to jerk open their curtains, just far enough to stick their heads out. Seeing four armed and masked men standing in the aisle was a terrifying experience, and some gasped with fear. Others called out.

"What's going on?"

"What's happening?"

"Who are you?"

"Sorry 'bout this unscheduled stop, folks," Loomis said, waving his pistol about. "But we need to do a little business with you."

"Business? What kind of business?" a male passenger asked.

"Money business," Loomis said. "All of you, open your curtains."

A few opened their curtains only marginally wider.

"Not good enough," Loomis said. "I want them opened wide. Open 'em all the way, or I'm going to start shooting. And the first place I'll shoot is into the berth that doesn't have the curtains open."

At that moment, the porter happened into the car and, seeing the commotion and the armed men, yelled.

"Who are you men? What are you doing in here? You can't be in this car!"

Loomis shot the porter, and the white-haired black man fell back amid screams from the passengers. One of the passengers, still wearing his sleeping gown, jumped down from his berth to see to the porter.

"He's dead," he said.

"Oh, my God!" a woman said.

The acrid smell of gun smoke filled the car and Loomis waved his pistol around. A little wisp of smoke was still curling from the gun barrel.

"I guess now that you folks know I mean business," he said. He pulled out his little cloth bag and handed it to the passenger who had gone to attend to the porter. "Put all your money in that bag."

"See here, this is unheard of!" the passenger sputtered. "I will not . . ."

That was as far as he got before Loomis brought his pistol down, sharply, on the man's head. The man collapsed across the porter's body.

The car was filled with gasps of amazement, but they were rather subdued because nobody wanted to get Loomis's attention.

"You," Loomis said, pointing to one of the other passengers. "Look around in this fella's berth and bring out all his money."

"What if he doesn't have any money?"

"You'd better pray that he does have some money," Loomis said. " 'Cause if he don't have any, I'm goin' to kill you."

It took but a moment for the passenger to find the money, which he quickly handed over to Loomis.

"Now, that's more like it," Loomis said. "And put your own money in the poke as well," he added.

After that, all the passengers began cooperating so that, within moments, the money bag was full.

"You folks did that just real well," Loomis said. "Now, there's one more thing we need before we go."

"What else is there? You've taken all our money," one of the women passengers said.

"Which ones of you are the MacCallisters?"

"Why do you want to know that?"

"Let's just say I want them to do a private show for us. Now, which ones of you are the MacCallisters?"

When nobody responded, Loomis pointed his pistol at the head of one of the women.

"I'm going to count to five," Loomis said. "If I don't find out which ones of you are the MacCallisters by the time I get to five, I'm going to kill this woman. Then, I'm going to start counting to five again, and kill someone else. And I'll keep on killin' in here until I find what I'm looking for."

"One."

"You're mad! You wouldn't do that!"

"Two."

"You're insane! There are other people on this train! You'll never get away with it."

"Three."

"No, please!" the woman begged. "Who are you? What are you doing?"

"Four," Loomis said, and this time he cocked the pistol.

"I'm Andrew MacCallister," Andrew said. Like the other passengers, he was dressed in a sleeping gown.

"I thought this would bring you out," Loomis said. Lowering the hammer on his pistol, he signaled for the others to move toward Andrew.

"What do you want with me?"

"Where is your sister?" Loomis asked.

"You've got me, that's enough. You can't have my sister, too."

"That's all right," Loomis said. "If you really feel that way, I'll just start killin' all the women in here until I get the right one."

"I'm the one you seek," a woman's voice announced very clearly.

Loomis chuckled. "I'm the one you seek," he repeated. "Lord, you folks do talk fancy, don't you? You got 'ny clothes with you?"

"They're in the baggage car," Andrew said.

"Then put on what you was wearin' before you climbed into the bed last night," Loomis ordered. "I don't care what you wear, just get dressed. The both of you."

"What do you want us to get dressed for?" Andrew asked.

"Because you're comin' with us."

"What makes you think we are going to come with you?" Andrew asked angrily.

Loomis pointed to the dead porter. "Do you want anyone else to die?"

"No," Andrew said.

"Then both of you get dressed, and hurry."

The curtains closed on the two berths, upper and lower, that were occupied by

Andrew and Rosanna. Then, just a few minutes later, they reopened and the two, now fully dressed, stepped out into the aisle.

The engineer blew the whistle.

"Hurry it up! We're fixin' to pull out!" Logan called.

Loomis took out a letter and dropped it on the floor of the train car.

"This here letter needs to go to a man named Falcon MacCallister back in Colorado Springs," he said. "I'm countin' on someone in this car gettin' it to him, 'cause if I don't hear from him in one week, I'll be killin' these two."

"Come on, hurry up! The train is moving!" Kelly said.

"All right, let's go," Loomis said, shoving his two prisoners toward the end of the car. The train was already rolling by the time they reached the vestibule, but Loomis pushed Andrew and Rosanna off, then jumped off behind them.

By the time all were down, the train was rolling at a pretty good clip and pulling away from them. Loomis took his hood off and the others followed suit.

"What do you want with us?" Andrew asked.

"You two just do what I say, and quit

askin' so damn many questions," Loomis replied.

The horses were no more than one hundred yards away from the track.

"Michaels!" Loomis called. "Michaels, where the hell are you?"

"I'm right here," the albino said, riding up from the shadows. He was riding one horse, and leading six others.

Seeing him, Rosanna gasped. The albino's pasty complexion was even whiter in the moonlight, and he looked for all the world like a ghost.

Strayhorn chuckled. "What's the matter? You scared of the albino?"

"No," Rosanna said. "No I was just — startled is all."

"Yeah, he does that to folks," Strayhorn said.

"Can you ride?" Loomis asked.

"Yes, a little."

"A little, huh?" Loomis said. "Well, you're going to have to ride more than just a little. Get mounted, the two of you."

Andrew started to mount one of the horses, but Loomis stopped him.

"No, let the woman have the mare. She's a mite more gentle. The woman can ride, can't she?"

Andrew gave the reins to Rosanna, then

chose the other horse. "Yes, she can ride," Andrew said, answering Loomis's question. He started to tell them that she was a champion rider, but thought better of it, believing that the less information he shared with them at this point, the better off they would be.

"Yeah, but can she ride without falling off the horse, is what I want to know."

"I'll hang on tight," Rosanna said as she mounted the horse, then arranged her dress in a position that would allow her to ride astride.

"Yeah, well you better hang on real tight, little lady," Loomis said. " 'Cause if you fall off, I'll tie a rope around you and drag you to where we're goin'."

"Whooeee, that come off slick as a whistle," Strayhorn said. "Wonder how much money we got."

"More'n a hunnert dollars, for sure," Logan said.

"When I say, we're going to divide it up," Loomis answered. "But that ain't nothin' compared to what we're goin' to get."

By now the puffing sound of the train was barely audible, and the long, lonesome sound of the whistle indicated just how far away the train was.

Rosanna shuddered.

Where were they, who were these men, and what was going to happen to them?

Rosanna watched as the man with the drooping eye took a rope from his saddle. The rope had been pre-tied with a loop on each end. He looped one end of it around her neck, and the other around Andrew's neck.

"All right," he said. "Let's ride."

As soon as the train got under way again, one of the passengers looked out onto the front vestibule, while another looked out back.

"They're gone!" the man up front said.

"Nobody back here either," the other said.

"Somebody needs to get the conductor."

"Get me for what?" the conductor asked, coming into the car at that moment. "What's going on here, why is everyone out of . . . ?" The conductor stopped in mid-sentence when he saw the porter lying on the floor of the car. "Travis!" he shouted, moving quickly to him.

"The porter is dead," one of the passengers said as the conductor knelt down to examine him.

"Who did this?"

"Some men."

"Some men? What men? What did they look like?"

"They were all wearin' masks."

" 'Tweren't masks, it was hoods they was wearin'," another said. "It covered their whole face, like this." He put his hand over his face in demonstration.

"Well, were they already on the train? Did anyone see them before they put on their hoods?"

"No, they come on when the train stopped."

"And they took the MacCallisters," another passenger said.

"The MacCallisters are gone?"

At the conductor's questions, everyone in the car started talking at the same time, so the conductor pointed to the first man.

"What is your name?" the conductor asked.

"Carl Taylor."

"Well, Mr. Taylor, how about you" — he looked at the other passengers — "and only you, tell me, in detail, just what the Sam Hill happened in here!"

While Taylor related the entire story, the other passengers nodded in agreement with what was being said. Then, when Taylor was finished, the conductor reached up and pulled on the emergency cord.

■ ■ ■ ■

When the conductor pulled the emergency cord, all the air brakes were immediately activated. The wheels locked and slid along the tracks, sending out showers of sparks.

In the engine, the fireman was thrown off balance and nearly fell against the hot furnace.

"What the hell, Doodle! You need to give me a warnin' when you're goin' to do somethin' like that."

"I didn't do it," Doodle answered, closing the valve to stop steam from going into the actuating cylinders. "It had to be someone on the train, pulling the emergency brake cord. Take a look on your side, Austin, see if you see anything."

With the fireman looking out one side and the engineer out the other, the train came to an emergency halt. It sat on the track then, still but not quiet, as the relief valves opened and closed.

"Here comes Paul," Doodle said as he saw the conductor running up alongside the train.

"Wonder what he wants," Austin mused.

"Doodle, we have to go back!" the conductor called up to him.

"Go back? Go back to where?"

"Go back to where we took on water! Some men came on board back at the water tower. They robbed the passengers in the Pullman car and they killed Travis."

"Why should we go back?" Doodle asked. "Seems to me like we should just report it at the next stop."

Paul shook his head. "No, we have to go back. They took the MacCallisters."

"The MacCallisters? That's them actors, ain't it?"

"Yes," Paul answered. "And if we lose them, the railroad will never hear the end of it, and neither will we."

"What would they have taken them for?" Doodle asked.

"I figure maybe just to keep someone on the train from shootin' at 'em when they got off. More'n likely the MacCallisters is still there. That's why we have to go back."

"All right," Doodle said. "Get back on board. We'll go back."

Fifteen minutes later, the train was, once again, sitting on the track beside the water tower. By now all the passengers, not just those in the Pullman car, knew about the men coming on board and taking the Mac-Callisters.

"I'll bet there's a reward for findin' 'em," someone suggested, and that was enough to spur several of them into leaving the train to help look around in the dark for them. Using hand-carried lanterns, they searched for nearly half an hour, but found nothing.

As they were searching for the two missing passengers, the conductor and the express man moved Travis's body from the aisle of the Pullman car into the baggage car.

"Thanks, McCorkle," Paul said.

"Yeah, well, I hate it that happened to poor old Travis, but you're right, we couldn't just leave him in the aisle of the car. It would upset the passengers somethin' fierce."

Paul had just jumped down from the baggage car when Doodle leaned out of the engine cab and called down to him.

"Paul, you better get everyone back on board."

"Give them just a few more minutes," Paul said. "The MacCallisters must be here somewhere."

Doodle shook his head. "Don't matter if they're here or not, we got to get goin'. There's another train due here in half an hour. We're going to need to open up a lead on them."

"Yeah," Paul said. "All right, I'll spread the word. How 'bout you givin' a toot on the whistle?"

Doodle nodded, pulled his head back into the engine, and a second later blew the whistle.

"All right, folks, that's all," Paul called to the searchers. "Let's get back on the train. Pass the word to the others. Back on the train. Doodle, give a couple of whistles."

Doodle climbed back onto the engine and blew the whistle a couple more times, and that had the effect of calling everyone back.

"Oh, say, conductor," one of the Pullman passengers said. "The leader of the men left a letter."

"He left a letter? Why didn't someone tell me before now?"

"I don't know. I forgot in all the excitement, I guess."

"Where is the letter?"

"I think Mr. Taylor has it," the passenger said, pointing to one of the other Pullman passengers.

"Thanks," Paul said. Then he called out to the other passenger. "Mr. Taylor! What's this I hear about the train robbers leavin' a letter?"

"Oh, yes," Taylor said, reaching into his pocket. "Here it is."

"Well, were you going to give it to me? Or were you going to maybe keep it as a souvenir?"

"Actually, I was goin' to turn it in at the next stop," Taylor said. "The robbers said that this was supposed to go to Falcon MacCallister in Colorado Springs."

"All right," Paul said. "I'll make certain that it gets on the next train going back."

Paul waited until the last passenger was aboard. Then he raised and lowered his lantern a couple of times to signal to the engineer that it was all right to go. He climbed aboard, just as the brakes were released and the train started forward.

CHAPTER FOURTEEN

Loomis and the others rode through the night, with Andrew and Rosanna riding very carefully because the looped rope ran from Andrew's neck to Rosanna's. If either of them fell while riding, it would probably kill both of them.

It was still dark when they finally stopped. Looking around, Andrew and Rosanna saw a main house, a barn, and a rather large corral.

"What is this place? A ranch, do you think?" Rosanna asked quietly.

"If it is, it's deserted," Andrew answered just as quietly.

They weren't quiet enough, because the albino heard them. "Shut up, you two. If we want you to talk, we'll ask you somethin'."

"What is this place?" Rosanna asked.

"It's a place where nobody will find you," the albino said. "Now, get down."

Rosanna started to dismount.

"Rosanna, wait!" Andrew called, stopping her just as she began. "We have to do it together, remember?"

"Oh, yes," Rosanna said. "I nearly forgot."

Coordinating their movements, the brother and sister dismounted, then waited to have the rope removed from their necks.

"Go on inside," the albino ordered gruffly.

"Wait, better let me go in first and have a look around," Strayhorn said, stepping up onto the porch.

The top hinge of the door was broken and when Strayhorn pushed to open it, the top of the door went in and the bottom of the door came out; then the entire door fell in with a crash, raising a cloud of dust.

"I don't reckon there is anyone home," Strayhorn said with a giggle. He started inside, then called out in pain and anger.

"Shit!"

"What is it? What happened?"

"I stepped on a nail," Strayhorn complained.

"We better get some light in here, or else we'll all be steppin' on nails and comin' down with the lockjaw," Logan said. Striking a match, he examined the inside of the room by the flickering light until he saw a candle. It took a second match for the candle to be lit, but they were rewarded with

175

a soft, golden bubble of light that pushed back the darkness.

The light of the candle also disclosed a sign, making them aware of where they were.

GOPHER CREEK STAGECOACH WAY-STATION
Hot Meals – 15 cents
Lester Truegood — Manager.

"Wouldn't mind having me one of them hot meals right now," Logan said.

"Tie them onto them two bunks over there," Loomis ordered, pointing to two bunks that were in line, head to head.

"Get in them bunks," Kelly ordered, and as Andrew and Rosanna complied, Kelly began tying them both to the beds and to each other.

"You needn't pull the rope so tightly around my wrists," Andrew said. "That hurts."

"Quit your bellyachin'," Kelly said as he continued to tie them to the bunks. "You don't hear your sister complainin', do you?"

"Would it do any good to complain?" Rosanna asked.

Kelly chuckled. "Not a bit," he said.

The blankets on the bed were of an exceptionally rough texture, almost like burlap bags. And the smells were horrible, a mélange of fetid, sour, and unpleasant aromas as if every meal ever cooked in this room had suddenly joined forces in one great, fetid odor.

"Loomis, may I ask you a question?" Andrew asked.

Loomis looked surprised. "How is it that you know my name?"

"I heard the men call you Loomis," Andrew said. "You seem to be the leader of this band of brigands."

"I'm the leader of a band of brigands, am I?" Loomis asked. He chuckled. "Yeah, I like that. I guess I am the leader of this band of — brigands." He set the word "brigands" apart from the rest of the sentence. "All right, what is your question?"

"Why have you brought us here?" Rosanna asked. "And what do you plan to do with us?"

"That's two questions," Loomis said. "But if you must know, I brought you here in order to hold you for ransom."

"Ransom? Ransom for what?" Rosanna asked.

"Well, now, that leads into your second question, as to what do I plan to do with you. Because if your brother decides not bring the money to pay for your freedom, what I intend to do with you is kill you both."

Three things that Falcon really enjoyed in life were good cigars, good whiskey, and a good poker game. Of course, his likes weren't limited to just those three things, but they certainly ranked high on his list and all three were available, in abundance, right here in Colorado Springs.

Falcon had not planned to stay after his brother and sister returned to New York. Yet here it was, at least four days after they left, and he was still in Colorado Springs. More specifically, he was still at the Broadmoor, enjoying the supply of cigars, whiskey, and cards.

At the moment, he was enjoying all three at the same time because he was puffing on a Cuban cigar, sipping a good Kentucky bourbon, and studying the hand he was holding.

The question before him was, should he break up his pair of jacks and draw one card to go for a flush, or keep the jacks and draw three new cards?

He decided to draw three new cards.

The first card he drew was a heart, which would have made his flush. He groaned inwardly. He drew two sevens, giving him two pair.

Two pair wasn't good enough, and he smiled graciously as the winner raked in his pot.

"Mr. MacCallister?" someone called from the door of the card room. "Is there a Falcon MacCallister in here?"

"Yes, I'm here," Falcon said, holding up his hand.

A young boy, about sixteen, hurried across the room to him. The boy was a messenger, one of many young boys who earned money by carrying messages between businesses and individuals in Colorado Springs.

"This come in on the train today," the boy said. "I was told to give it to you."

"Thanks," Falcon said. He picked up a dollar chip from his pile and gave it to the boy.

"Gee! Thanks, mister!" the messenger boy said.

Falcon saw that his name on the letter was misspelled as Macalester, and he remembered that Loomis Tate had misspelled it that way. With a sense of foreboding, he opened the letter.

MACALESTER
IV GOT YUR BROTHER AND SISTER

*AND IM GOING TO KEEP THEM UNTIL
YOU GIV ME $20,000. COME TO THE
LONG TRAIL SALOON IN EAGLE TAIL
KANSAS AT 4 PM ON THE 9TH. BRING
MONEY. SOMEONE WILL MET YOU
THER AND TELL YOU WHAT TO DO
NEXT.*

Falcon folded the letter, then drummed his fingers on the table for a moment.

"Bad news?" one of the other players asked.

"What?" Falcon asked, looking up.

"The letter," the player said, pointing toward the message Falcon had received. "You look troubled. Is it bad news?"

"I don't know yet," Falcon said. "But there is a chance that it may be. Gentlemen, I have very much enjoyed our game, but if you will excuse me, I'm afraid I must cash in and leave."

"It has been most enjoyable," the man who won the last hand said. "It is always good to play cards with a gracious loser."

"He's just as gracious a winner," one of the other players said. "He won more last night than he has lost tonight."

"Well, then, that truly does make him a credit to the game."

Falcon took his chips to the cashier to

exchange them for cash. As he was waiting, Pourtales came up to talk to him.

"Leaving the tables early tonight, Falcon?" Pourtales asked.

"Yes," Falcon said. Falcon reached into his inside jacket pocket. "James, I wonder if I could ask a favor of you." He pulled out a book of blank bank drafts, and began writing on one.

"Of course you can," Pourtales replied. "After all you have done for me in the last few weeks, I will do anything it is in my power to do."

Falcon finished writing the draft, blew on the ink to dry it, then handed it Pourtales.

"The bank has closed for the day," he said. "I wonder if you could cash this for me."

Pourtales chuckled. "I'd be glad to," he said. "Running a little short of spending money, are you? I'll just give this to . . ." Pourtales looked at the check for the first time, then gasped in surprise.

"Falcon, this draft is drawn for twenty thousand dollars," he said.

"Yes."

"*Gott im Himmel,* Falcon, surely you have not lost so much at the gambling tables. I would feel very bad."

Falcon smiled. "Do not worry, my friend. The tables have not been overly generous to me, but I have won more than I have lost. No, this is for . . ." Falcon paused for a moment, then showed Pourtales the letter.

Pourtales read it, then hit his fist in his hand. "No!" he said. "This is my fault! It would not have happened if I had not brought them out here."

"You didn't bring them out here, James," Falcon said. "They are both grown up now. They brought themselves."

"Of course I will cash your draft," Pourtales said, taking the instrument. "I just hate to see you pay those cretins."

"Who said I'm going to pay them?" Falcon asked.

"But the draft?"

"Have you ever gone trapping, James?" Falcon asked.

"Trapping?"

"Yes, for beaver, muskrat, wolves, weasels," Falcon said.

"No, I can't say that I have," Pourtales replied.

"Funny thing about running a trapline. In order to get the critter into the trap, you need bait."

"Bait?" Pourtales said with a puzzled expression on his face. Then he smiled broadly and laughed out loud. "Yes, bait." He handed the draft to his cashier, and the cashier began counting out the money.

"Tate wants me in Eagle Tail on the ninth," Falcon said. "If I take the train out tonight, I will reach Eagle Tail late on the evening of the eighth."

"That's almost a full day ahead of time," Pourtales said.

"Yes."

"Why so early?"

Falcon smiled. "Another thing about setting out a trapline is to make sure you get there before the varmint does."

Pourtales smiled. "I almost feel sorry for the varmint," he said.

"Here you are, sir, twenty thousand dollars," the cashier said, stacking the money up on the counter in front of the window.

"You'll need something to carry that in," Pourtales offered. "I have a leather valise, let me get it for you."

"No need," Falcon said. He pointed to a cloth bag. "That will do, if you can spare it."

"Of course, anything," Pourtales said, pointing it out to the cashier, who picked it up.

"Thanks," Falcon said as he began filling the sack with money.

"Falcon, would you like me to go with you?"

"No," Falcon said. "The fewer people there are to set a trapline, the more effective the trapline is."

"Gott ist mit Ihnen," Pourtales said, reaching out to shake Falcon's hand.

"Thank you," Falcon said.

With a final nod of good-bye, Falcon left the casino, carrying the nondescript cloth bag that contained twenty thousand dollars in cash.

"Do you wish to check your bags through?" the ticket clerk asked.

"No," Falcon said, throwing the saddle-bags, into which he had transferred the money, over his shoulder. "Just make certain that my saddle stays with the horse."

"It's all taken care of," the clerk said.

As Falcon waited for the train, he saw people beginning to gather at the station. The uninitiated might think that they were all passengers, or were meeting, or seeing off, passengers, but Falcon knew better. He understood that one of the most important events in any Western town was the arrival of a train. Many would come to watch the trains even if they had no personal stake in their arrivals or departures. And as the townspeople began to gather, the crowd would take on a carnival atmosphere, with a great deal of laughing and joking.

Falcon found a place away from the jostling crowd. Then, leaning against the depot wall, he lit a cheroot and smoked quietly as he waited.

"Here comes the train!" someone shouted.

Immediately upon the heels of the shout, came the sound of the train whistle, announcing its arrival.

"It's right on time tonight," another said.

The laughing and joking ceased as everyone grew quiet to await the train's arrival.

Falcon watched as the people on the platform moved closer to the track to stare in the direction from which the train would come. In the distance they could see the headlamp, which was a gas flame and mirror reflector, casting a long, bright beam in front of the oncoming train.

The train could be heard quite clearly now, not only the whistle but the hollow sounds of the puffing steam coming from the engine, then rolling back as an echo from the surrounding hillsides. As the train drew even closer, Falcon could see glowing sparks spewing out from the smokestack, whipped up by the billowing clouds of smoke.

The train pounded into the station with

sparks flying from the drive wheels and glowing hot embers dripping from its firebox. Following the engine and tender were the golden patches of light that were the windows of the passenger cars. The train squealed to a halt. Then, inside, Falcon could see the people who would be getting off here beginning to move toward the exits at the ends of the cars.

He walked down to the end of the platform, next to the stock car, and watched as two horses were off-loaded. One of the baggage men stood by, holding Falcon's horse. As soon as the two horses were led down the ramp, Falcon's horse was led up the ramp.

Falcon started to remind them not to forget his saddle, but that wasn't necessary because even as his horse was being led up the ramp, another employee came out of the depot carrying the saddle.

With his horse and saddle safely loaded, Falcon boarded the train. He walked down the aisle of the car until he found a seat at the rear of the car.

Sitting in his seat, he put the saddlebags beside him, then pulled out the letter from Tate and read it again.

"Tate, if anything happens to my brother or sister, I'll kill you," he said, speaking very quietly. Then he added, "No, on second thought, I'm going to kill you no matter what."

"I beg your pardon, sir?" the conductor asked, passing by at that moment.

Falcon smiled at him. "Sorry," he said. "I'm so used to talking to my horse that I sometimes forget I'm just talking to myself."

The conductor chuckled. "Yes, sir, I know what you mean." He took Falcon's ticket, punched it, then handed it back. He pointed to the saddlebags beside him.

"Would you like me to put those bags in the overhead for you?"

"No, thank you," Falcon said. He pulled them closer to him. "They're fine right here."

"Very good, sir," the conductor replied as he moved on up the car to check the tickets of the others who had just boarded.

CHAPTER FIFTEEN

For a while, the candle continued to burn, and Andrew found himself watching the flickering shadows on the wall near the two bunks where he and Rosanna were being held. Because of the way he was tied in the bunk, none of the ones who had brought them here were visible. He could, however, see their shadows, cast on the wall by the candle flame.

He was beginning to get cramps in his arms, a stiffening of his neck, and a growing pain in his back. He tried to stretch and move his body in a way that would give him some relief, and though it helped some, it didn't do much to alleviate his discomfort.

He could hear a couple of his captors talking, though they were talking so quietly that he couldn't understand what they were saying. He also knew that some of them were asleep, because he could hear them snoring.

"Rosanna," he whispered. "Rosanna, are

you awake?"

"Yes, I'm awake," Rosanna replied. "Who can sleep like this?"

"Yeah, I know what you mean. My back is killing me."

"Andrew?"

"Yes."

"If you get a chance to escape, take it. Don't wait for me."

"No, I couldn't do that," Andrew replied. "There's no way I'm going to leave you behind."

"I'm not asking you to leave me behind," Rosanna said. "I'm asking you to escape for both of us. If you get away, then you can get help."

"Yes," Andrew said. "Yes, I see what you mean. But they may not be watching you as closely as they watch me. So the same applies to you. If you get a chance to get away, you take it."

"You two stop your gabbin' over there," Loomis called.

Andrew felt his twin sister working against the restraining ropes until she managed to touch his hand with hers. He squeezed her hand and she squeezed back. It had always been like this between them. Though obviously not identical twins, they were as close as identical twins, and were often able to

189

communicate without talking.

They lay in silence for another several minutes as, gradually, it began to grow lighter. Then, when it was light enough to see quite clearly, Loomis came across the floor to stand over the bunks and stare down at them.

"We're goin' out to the corral to check on the horses," Loomis said. "Don't you two try nothin' while we are gone."

"Are you going to feed us anything?" Andrew asked.

"Yeah, sure, I'm going to feed you. Your brother ain't goin' to pay money for you if you ain't alive."

"Falcon isn't going to pay you any money, anyway," Andrew said.

"Sure he will."

"No, he won't," Andrew said.

"You're his own brother and sister. Are you tellin' me that he ain't goin' to pay money to save his own brother and sister?"

"Yes, that's exactly what I'm telling you," Andrew said.

"You better hope he does pay," Loomis said. " 'Cause if the son of a bitch don't pay, I will kill the both of you."

"And if he does pay, you will let us go?" Andrew asked. It wasn't a pleading question, it was a sarcastic question, indicating that Andrew believed that Loomis Tate had no intention of letting them go, regardless of whether Falcon paid or not.

"He'd just better pay, that's all," Loomis said without answering Andrew directly.

"How long are you going to leave us tied up?" Rosanna asked. She pulled and strained against the ropes. "Because I have to tell you, this is most uncomfortable."

Loomis stroked his chin for a moment as if considering her question.

"Me 'n the others is goin' outside for a few minutes to check the horses and such, so there won't be anybody to watch you. But I'll untie you when we get back in."

"Why not untie us now?" Rosanna said. "There are five of you and only two of us. You are armed and we aren't. Where are we going to go? How are we going to get away?"

Loomis looked as if he were actually considering it for a moment; then he thought better of it.

"No," he said. "I'll untie you when we get back in."

Walking away from the two bunks, Loomis signaled to the others to follow him outside.

They ambled over to the corral, where Strayhorn and Kelly began urinating.

"Woowee, I had to piss like a Russian

191

racehorse," Strayhorn said.

"I'll tell you what, that is one good-lookin' woman in there," Logan said. "I don't believe I've ever seen anyone that pretty."

"Yeah, well, don't get to thinkin' on that too hard," Loomis said. " 'Cause she ain't goin' to be around all that long."

"So you think MacCallister will show up with the money?" Logan asked. "I mean, I heard what they told you in there, how's they don't think he will pay the money."

"Oh, he'll show up with the money, all right," Loomis said.

"How do you know he will?" Logan asked. "I mean, especially since they're so sure he won't."

"That's 'cause they're a couple of city dudes who don't know nothin'," Loomis answered. "They think I'm runnin' a bluff, but MacCallister knows better. He knows I'll kill his brother and sister if he don't come up with the money."

"So if he does show up with the money, how do we handle it?"

"How do we handle what?"

"How do we handle turnin' them over to him? I mean, do we just tell him where we're keepin' 'em, or what?" Strayhorn asked.

Loomis's laughter was coarse and hollow.

192

"Hell, it won't make no difference to him where they are, 'cause we ain't tellin' him nothin'," Loomis said. "I aim to kill Mr. Falcon MacCallister just as soon as I get the money."

"What for?" Logan asked. "I mean, if we get the money, why are you going to kill him?"

"For one thing, I'm going to kill him because the son of a bitch killed my brother," Loomis said. "You do remember that, don't you?"

"Yeah, sure, I remember it."

"And for another, I'm going to kill him because he wouldn't let it go at that. Soon as he got his brother and sister back, he'd come after us to get his money back. And I don't want to be looking over my shoulder for the rest of my life just to see if he's back there doggin' us."

"Yeah," Logan said. "Yeah, I can understand that, I suppose. But what about the two back there in the house? I mean, after we've kilt their brother and took the money, what are we goin' to do with them? You goin' to let them go?"

"That's a good question, and I been thinkin' a lot about that," Loomis said.

"So, have you come up with an answer? What are we goin' to do?"

"After we get the money, then we're goin' to have to kill them, too," Loomis said. "I don't see no other way of handlin' it."

"I don't know if we want to do that, Loomis," Kelly said.

"Why not?"

"Well, just think about it. Their names is in the paper all the time. Folks go see 'em doin' their plays and such. They're real famous. If something happens to them, everyone is going to be looking."

"Uh-huh. Looking for who?"

"Well, for us."

"No," Loomis said. "They'll be looking for the ones who done it."

Kelly looked at Loomis as if he had lost his senses. "Well, hell, Loomis, that's what I said."

"No, you said they were going to be lookin' for us. But they ain't goin' to be lookin' for us 'cause they won't know that we are the ones that done it. We was all wearin' masks, remember?"

"Yeah, but you left that note for MacCallister. What if someone on the train read it?"

"More'n likely they did read it," Loomis said. "But I didn't sign it. Not even MacCallister will know who we are. He'll just know that somebody has taken his brother and sister, and if he wants to see them alive again, he's goin' to have to pay us the money we asked him for."

"That will be fine until he sees us," Logan said. "Don't forget, he knows ever'one of us."

"Which is exactly why we're goin' to kill him," Loomis said.

Logan paused for a moment, then nodded. "Yeah," he said. "Yeah, I guess you're right."

"And that's also why we're goin' to have to kill them two back in there." Loomis pointed toward the house. "Do you think if we let them go that it would be the end of it? No, sir, it would not be the end of it," Loomis said, answering his own question. "It's because they're famous that they'll be able to get ever'one to listen to them. I mean, we come here from no farther than Colorado and yet no one has ever heard of us. But if we let them two in there go, they'll get to blabbin' and the next thing you know, folks will know about us from California to New York. We won't be able to go anywhere."

"Why, we'd be as famous as Billy the Kid," Strayhorn said with a big smile.

"Yeah, as famous as Billy the Kid. And

you seen what happened to him, didn't you?"

"Oh, yeah," Strayhorn said. "Yeah, I see what you mean."

"What about you, Kelly?" Loomis asked his brother.

Kelly nodded. "I hate to kill someone so pretty, but I guess you're right. It has to be done."

"Come on, let's get back inside," Loomis said. "Logan, you can cook breakfast for us."

"Why me?" Logan asked.

"Because I told you to," Loomis replied.

The five men tramped back into the house, then looked over to the corner where Andrew and Rosanna lay, still tied to the bunks.

"Will you untie us now?" Andrew asked.

"Will you give me your word that you won't try and escape?" Loomis asked.

"As my sister said, there are five of you, and you are all armed," Andrew said. "Besides, you have not even given us the opportunity to relieve ourselves."

"Yeah, all right, untie 'em," Loomis ordered, and Logan went over to untie them.

"Thank you," Rosanna said as she sat up on the bed, rubbing her wrists. "Now, may

I please go attend to my — uh — personal needs?"

"Go ahead, but you'd better take a good look around in the privy when you get out there," Loomis said. "This place has been abandoned ever since the railroad come through, and like as not there's scorpions and snakes and all sorts of critters out there."

"I've dealt with such things before," Rosanna said. She started toward the door.

"Wait," Loomis called to her.

Rosanna stopped.

"I don't want you to go out by yourself. Strayhorn, you go with her. Keep an eye on her."

Strayhorn smiled broadly. "Keep an eye on her, right. I'll do just that," he said. "Come along, girlie, you won't have to be worryin' none about them critters long as I'm in there with you."

"What do you mean, as long as you are in there with me?" Rosanna asked sharply.

"You heard what Loomis said," Strayhorn replied. "He wants me to keep an eye on you."

"For cryin' out loud, Strayhorn, I don't mean for you to go into the privy with her. Just keep an eye on her from outside."

"Oh, hell," Strayhorn said. "Look, don't

you think it would be better if I went in with her? I mean, that way we know she wouldn't try nothin', and I could look out for the critters for her. We wouldn't want her to get bit or nothin'."

"She'll be just fine in there by herself. You stay outside the privy," Loomis said.

"All right, whatever you say," Strayhorn said, obviously disappointed

Despite Loomis's warning, Rosanna saw no scorpions or snakes. She did see Strayhorn's eye looking through a crack, though, and reaching down, she picked up a handful of dirt, then threw it at the crack.

When she stepped outside a moment later, she saw Strayhorn, still rubbing at his eye, which was now red.

"Oh, did something get in your eye, Mr. Strayhorn?" she asked sweetly.

"Get on back inside," Strayhorn growled.

CHAPTER SIXTEEN

It was now early evening of the second day, and Falcon was in the dining car. He had changed trains in Denver, transferring from the Denver and Rio Grande Line to the Union Pacific. He had not taken a Pullman or a parlor car for this part of the trip because he would be getting off later tonight.

"Anything else I can get you, sir?" a white-jacketed steward asked, approaching Falcon's table.

Falcon, who had just enjoyed a dinner of elk steak, minted green peas, and baked sweet potato, picked up the napkin and dabbed at his lips.

"No, thank you. My compliments to the chef — it was an excellent dinner."

"Thank you, sir, I'm sure he will be very pleased," the steward said.

Picking up his saddlebags, Falcon returned to his car. He sat there for a moment, looking through the window at the little yellow patches of lights that were sliding by on the ground beside him at better than twenty miles per hour. Then, crossing his arms around the strap of his saddlebags, Falcon tipped his hat forward, leaned back in his chair, and went to sleep.

The dream came almost immediately.

Falcon pushed open the batwing doors and stepped inside the saloon, standing for a moment to let his eyes adjust to the dark.

The men he was after were sitting at a far table, playing cards and sharing a bottle, but drinking very little.

Falcon walked up to the long bar and ordered a drink, conscious of the many eyes on him. He ignored the open stares, concentrating on his shot glass. Trouble would start soon enough, he felt. No need for him to hasten it.

All that changed when a local sidled up to his side and whispered, "You see that big feller at the end of the bar, mister?"

"Yes," Falcon returned in a whisper.

"He's been braggin' for several days. Ever'time he come into town. He claims to be one of the men who killed Jamie MacCallister."

Falcon felt a coldness wash over him. He lifted his eyes and stared down the bar at the man pointed out to him; a big burly fellow, with swarthy looks and a scar on one side of his face.

"What's his name?" Falcon asked the local.

"I heard him called Rud a time or two."

Falcon motioned for the bartender and told him to give the citizen a drink. The drink poured, Falcon said, "You'd better drink that and then get out of the way."

"Yes, sir. Thank you." The citizen gulped down the bourbon and walked off to a far corner of the huge first floor of the Stampede Saloon.

Falcon brushed back his coat, exposing both .44s, and stepped away from the bar. "I hear tell there's a man here claims to have killed Jamie MacCallister," he spoke in a loud voice.

"I killed Jamie MacCallister," the swarthy man said, stepping away from the far end of the bar. "It was a fair fight."

"You're a liar. Way I heard it, Jamie MacCallister was shot in the back. Twice, with a rifle."

"No man calls me a liar, mister."

"I just did," Falcon said. "I knew Jamie Mac-Callister. No two-bit loudmouth like you would have had the courage to stand up and hook and draw against a man like him. So that makes you a liar and a back-shooting murderer."

"I was there, mister. I faced MacCallister and

201

shot him dead. So you can take your mouth and go to hell, or drag iron."

"Make your play, back-shooter."

Rud cursed and went for his gun, and Falcon drilled him as his hand touched the butt of his .45. The bullet slammed into the center of the man's chest and knocked him back against the bar. He slowly sank to the floor, dead.

The piano player in the back of the room began three notes on the keyboard:

G–C–E

He played them over and over until they filled Falcon's mind.

Falcon woke up, felt the rhythm of the train, and heard the clack of wheels over rail joints. He also heard the same three notes he had been hearing in his dream.

G–C–E

The conductor was walking down the aisle of the car, striking a three-note xylophone, and that was what Falcon was hearing. It is also what had intruded into his dream.

G–C–E

"Eagle Tail, Kansas," the conductor was saying after each three-note series was struck. "Next stop is Eagle Tail, Kansas."

"Conductor," Falcon called as the conductor walked by his seat.

"Yes, sir, Mr. MacCallister?"

"You won't forget that I have a horse in the stock car. I wouldn't want the train to pull off with him."

"It's on our trip-log, Mr. MacCallister," the conductor said. "Trust me, we won't leave with your horse."

"Thanks."

The conductor nodded, then continued on through the car, striking the same three notes and repeating, over and over again: "Eagle Tail, Kansas."

G–C–E

"Next stop is Eagle Tail, Kansas."

Falcon's dream had been about an encounter he had during his mission to avenge the killing of his father, Jamie Ian MacCallister.[*] When he stopped to think about it, it didn't seem all that unusual that he would have dreamed about avenging his father. After all, that was what this trip was all about, wasn't it? The only difference was,

* *Rage of Eagles*

he didn't know if Andrew and Rosanna were alive or dead.

But as far as the vengeance was concerned, it didn't make any difference. He would have revenge, because he had already made up his mind to kill the kidnappers anyway.

Fifteen minutes later, Falcon was standing out on the depot platform in Eagle Tail. A large clock that hung down from one of the support braces of the platform roof said that it was nine-fifteen. Somehow, Falcon had thought it was much later than that. Perhaps because he had been sleeping, he had lost track of time. He watched as his horse was off-loaded; then he walked up to him.

"Now, that ride wasn't all that bad, was it?" he asked as he patted the horse gently on the neck. He took a lump of sugar from his jacket pocket and held it out in front of the horse. The horse, very delicately, picked up the cube of sugar with his extended lips.

"Mister, where do you want your saddle?" one of the baggage men asked.

"Bring it to me," Falcon said. "I'm going to ride him down to the livery to board him."

"No need to go that far unless you just want to," the baggage man said. "They can board your horse right here at the depot."

"That's good to know," Falcon said.

Shouldering the saddle himself, Falcon led the horse around to the other side of the depot, where he saw a small boarding stable. It appeared to be clean enough to satisfy him, and he was glad to see that, despite the late hour, there was someone working.

"I'd like to board my horse here," Falcon said.

"Twenty-five cents a night," the liveryman said, removing a piece of straw from his mouth while he spoke.

"All right."

"In advance."

"All right."

"And if you ain't here to claim him, or pay for another day by noon tomorrow, I'll turn him out."

"Here's for four days," Falcon said, handing the stableman a dollar.

"I'll keep an eye on your saddlebags for an extra ten cents a day," the stable keep offered.

"No, thanks," Falcon said. "I'll take care of them."

"Suit yourself," the man said, taking the reins of Falcon's horse and leading him toward the back.

With his horse seen to, Falcon decided to take a look around town, just to see what kind of place this was. He heard the engineer blow the whistle, then open the steam valve as the train began pulling away amidst the cacophony of whistles, bells, loud chugging, and final shouts of good-bye from those who had turned out to wish loved ones a safe journey.

As the noise of the train receded, the noise of a town at night took over. From one of the houses he could hear someone playing a piano, and playing it very well. The soothing music was offset by an argument ensuing from one of the other houses.

A mule began braying.

A freshening breeze caused a hanging sign to begin swinging and, with each swing, the wood squeaked in protest.

When Falcon stepped up onto the boardwalk, his boots drummed against the boards as he walked through the town.

Eagle Tail was laid out like the letter T with the cross of the T running parallel to the track. The road that ran perpendicular to the track was the main street, ending at the depot on the near end, and at a church on the far end. The church, empty at this time of night, glowed bright white in the light of the full moon.

In between those two anchors stood a mix of buildings including an apothecary, a dry goods store, a newspaper office, and a couple of saloons. There was also a Chinese laundry. Even though it was after normal business hours, Falcon could hear the singsong voices of Chinese men and women, carrying on animated conversations as they labored to have laundry ready for the next day.

As Falcon walked by the newspaper office, he saw that it, too, was lit up. The latest edition was tacked up outside for passersby to see, no doubt as a form of advertisement for the paper. The headline of the first column read:

MacCALLISTERS TAKEN FROM TRAIN!

Falcon stepped into the newspaper office and saw the editor working at his press. He forced the platen down and made the impression, then pulled the bed out, raised the tympan, lifted the sheet off the bed of type, then held it up and examined his work for a moment. It wasn't until that moment that the editor saw Falcon standing in his shop. Falcon's sudden, and unexpected, appearance startled the newspaperman and he jumped.

"Sir, the newspaper is closed for business at night," the editor said. "This is when I put out tomorrow's edition."

"I'm sorry, I didn't mean to frighten you."

"I wasn't frightened exactly," the editor said. "Just startled."

"At any rate, it is always good to see a free press at work," Falcon said from just inside the door.

"Indeed, sir, it is," the editor replied. "It was Thomas Jefferson himself who said, 'Given the choice of living in a country without a government or without a free press, I would choose to live without a government.' "

"That is true," Falcon said. "But isn't Jefferson also the one who said of the press that 'truth itself is polluted when it appears in the press'?"

The editor laughed, then wiped his hand on his apron before extending it in friendship.

"You know your history, sir. I'm Thomas Blanton, publisher and editor of the *Pronouncement,* at your service. I am also the reporter, printer, advertising salesman, delivery boy, and janitor."

"You sound like an entire staff," Falcon said.

"Indeed I am, sir. Indeed I am."

"The paper that you have out front," Falcon said. "Is that tomorrow's edition?"

"It is."

"I would like to buy an early copy if I might."

"I suppose that could be arranged. Is there a particular story that has caught your interest?"

"Yes, the story about the passengers who were taken from the train."

"You are talking about the MacCallisters," Blanton said. He shook his head slowly and made a clucking sound. "What a shame that is. They were such nice people. Why, did you know they took the time to leave the train and shake hands with just about everyone who had turned out to greet them?"

"Yes, well, Andrew and Rosanna always were the kind who sought attention," Falcon said. "In fact, I think they would die without it."

The smile left the editor's face. "That seems like a rather harsh observation to make," he said.

"Well, if I can't make a harsh observation, who can?" Falcon replied. "My name is Falcon MacCallister and Andrew and Rosanna are my brother and sister."

The editor beamed.

"Falcon MacCallister, you say!" he said. "Well, how fortunate it is to meet you. I do believe that your fame is every bit as great as that of your brother and sister. It is indeed an honor, sir, to have you in Eagle Tail."

"Thank you," Falcon said. "What have you learned about the disappearance of Andrew and Rosanna?"

"Learned?"

"You are a newspaperman, Mr. Blanton," Falcon said. "I'm certain that, by now, you have interviewed some of the passengers who were on the train that night, have you not?"

Blanton nodded. "Yes, as a matter of fact, I did interview them."

"If you don't mind sharing with me, I'd like to know everything you have found out about what happened," Falcon said.

"You're going after the kidnappers, aren't you?" Blanton asked.

"Yes."

"Well, I don't know who they are, but I can tell you —"

"Oh, I know who they are," Falcon said easily.

"What's that? You know who they are? But

how is that possible? Nobody could identify them."

"There were five of them; the two Tate brothers, Logan, Strayhorn, and Michaels. Michaels is an albino."

Blanton looked up quickly.

"An albino, you say?"

"Yes."

"I wonder if . . ." Blanton began. Then he finished with, "It has to be."

"What?" Falcon asked.

"I never put it together before," Blanton said. "But there were five men who came into Ziegenhorn's a couple of days ago — just the day before your brother and sister come through on the train, as it turns out. And one of 'em was an albino."

"That has to be them."

"Nobody said anything about an albino holding up the train," Blanton said. "But then, they were all wearing masks. And there were only four of them."

"Makes sense that there were only four," Falcon said. "They probably left one back to hold the horses."

"Yes, I hadn't thought of that," Blanton said. He looked back at his press, and at the unprinted pile of paper beside it.

"I'll tell you what," he said, taking off the apron. "I'll finish this print run later. What do you say you and I go down to Ziegen-horn's. He will be there, and I'm pretty sure Kingsley will be there as well."

"Ziegenhorn? Kingsley?"

"It's sort of a general store, café, and bunking house all at the same time. A man named Ziegenhorn owns the place," Blanton said. "And Crack Kingsley is our local marshal. They were there the other day when the albino and the others came through. Maybe if we all put our heads together, we can come up with something."

"Falcon MacCallister, huh?" Kingsley said. He extended his hand. "Well, I must say that I've heard about you and your famous pa. But I never thought I would meet you."

"Have a beer, Mr. MacCallister, on the house," Ziegenhorn offered.

"I will have a beer," Falcon said. "But I insist on paying for it, not just for mine, but for a round."

"Nope, you can't do that," Ziegenhorn said. "I don't have a license to sell liquor. All I can do is serve it to my friends."

"Well, in that case, I appreciate being regarded as your friend," Falcon said.

"I'm told that a group of men came through here the other day," Falcon said when Ziegenhorn returned with the beers.

"One of them was an albino."

"That's right," Ziegenhorn said. "I've seen albinos before, but I've never seen one like this fella. He was as white as a maggot."

"If they are who I think they are, it would be a bunch who escaped from jail back in Colorado Springs. In fact, they literally escaped from the hangman, because they were going to be hanged later that same day. Loomis Tate and . . ."

"Loomis! Yes, that's the name!" Kingsley said, interrupting Falcon and striking his hand with his fist. "One of them called the other Loomis. By damn, I thought I'd heard that name before."

"You said you was going to look it up," Ziegenhorn said.

"Yeah, I know," Kingsley said. "But what with all the excitement of the MacCallisters coming through, I forgot."

"Did Tate and the others know that my sister and brother were coming through?" Falcon asked.

"Yes, we told them. Well, we told everyone about it," Blanton said. "Oh, my God," he said, covering his mouth with his hand. "It's our fault, isn't it?"

"What's our fault?" Kingsley said. "What are you talking about?"

"The men that were here," Blanton said.

"We told them that the MacCallisters were coming through, and they are the ones who took the MacCallisters off the train."

"You're right, we did tell them," Ziegenhorn said. "Oh, Mr. MacCallister, I'm so sorry."

"Don't be ridiculous," Falcon said dismissively. "You did nothing wrong simply by telling them that Andrew and Rosanna were coming through here. They are the ones who took them off the train. They are the ones who are guilty."

"Is there anything we can do to help?" Kingsley asked.

"I don't know," Falcon said. "Maybe if we talk enough, we'll come up with something helpful."

"They were only riding five horses when they came through here," Blanton said. "But one of the passengers on the train insisted that he counted tracks for seven horses."

"That means they got two more horses somewhere," Falcon said. "Do you know if anyone is . . ."

"Landers," Blanton said. "Josh Landers."

"Who?" Kingsley asked.

"It's a story I ran a couple of days ago. Happened just north of here. Hank, you have Tuesday's paper?"

"Yeah, I think so," Ziegenhorn said. He

walked down to the far end of the counter, reached under it, then pulled out a paper. "Here it is," he said.

"Bring it here," Blanton said.

Ziegenhorn brought the paper back and Blanton handed it to Falcon. "Bottom story, left column," he said. "I didn't run it any bigger because it didn't happen in our county. Besides which, this is mostly a story I just took from another paper."

YOUTH MURDERED!
Horses Stolen.

WALLACE, KANSAS: News has reached the *Pronouncement* of a terrible crime committed just north of our fair city. According to a reliable source, Josh Landers, owner of a small farm, told the sheriff of St. Joseph County that his older son, Johnny, had been murdered by a band of men who rode through his property.

Landers said that Johnny and his younger son, Jesse, were swimming when the men came by and began taking the two boys' horses. Johnny, by all accounts a very brave young lad, confronted them and was shot and killed for his effort. Jesse, as resourceful as his brother was brave, hid from the murderous thugs by

215

lying on the bottom of the pond and breathing through a hollow reed.

Jesse was unable to describe any of the men, but stated that he believed one man was wearing a white hood over his face.

Jesse is eleven years old. Johnny, his brother who was killed, was fourteen.

"I remember reading that story," Ziegenhorn said. "I thought it was a tragic story, but I didn't make any sort of a connection between that and the MacCallisters being taken from the train."

"The white hood," Falcon said.

"I beg your pardon?"

"The boy said one of the men was wearing a white hood over his face."

"Yes, I noticed that. It seemed rather odd to me that only one would be masked," Ziegenhorn said.

"Unless the boy was too far away, and too frightened to see clearly," Falcon said. "In which case the white hood could be the white face of an albino."

"I'll be damned," Kingsley said. "You may have something there."

"But they took the horses from a couple of boys," Ziegenhorn said. "I mean, wouldn't you think they would take them from a ranch or something? They were taking a chance on what kind of horses they would be getting from a couple of young boys. Don't you think that, as far as quality is concerned, they would have more to choose from if they had taken them from a ranch?"

"No, that is precisely another reason why I think it might be Tate and his bunch," Falcon said. "They weren't interested in quality; they were interested in opportunity."

"Opportunity?" Kingsley said.

"Yes. They needed horses, the horses were there, it was a simple matter to just take them."

"All right, but why would they have killed the boy? And why did they try to kill the other one?" Ziegenhorn asked.

"When they came here, did any of you recognize them as wanted men?" Falcon asked.

"No."

"And they want to keep it that way. I think they killed the boy because he saw them, and could describe them. If they had robbed your store, Mr. Ziegenhorn, they would have killed all three of you as well."

"Oh, my," Ziegenhorn said, nervously pulling his shirt collar away from his neck. "Oh, my, I hadn't considered that."

"Which is why I believe that they have no intention of letting my brother and sister live, whether I give them the money or not," Falcon concluded.

"Damn," Ziegenhorn said. "That's not even something I want to think about."

"It's all right, our intentions even out," Falcon said with a humorless smile.

"What do you mean?" Blanton asked.

"I don't intend to let them live," Falcon said resolutely.

"So, what are you going to do now?" Kingsley asked.

"It's too late to do anything tonight, so I thought I'd find a saloon and have a few drinks, then get a room and spend the night. Tomorrow, I'll go out to the Landers farm and talk to the boy. Then I might see if I can pick up some tracks from there."

"Would you like me to go with you?" Kingsley asked.

"No, I work better by myself."

"All right," Kingsley replied, trying not to show how relieved he was at having his offer for help refused. "I really wouldn't have any jurisdiction there anyway. I'm a city marshal. You'd need to deal with the sheriff of St. Joseph County, or perhaps a United States marshal."

"I understand, but I don't intend to

218

bother them. I'll take care of this myself. Now, where's the nearest saloon?" Falcon asked.

"We have two," Ziegenhorn said. "I wouldn't recommend the Jayhawker, it's pretty rough. You might try the Long Trail, though."

"Long Trail," Falcon said. He nodded. "Thanks."

CHAPTER SEVENTEEN

Falcon had purposely left out mentioning anything about the note from Loomis telling him to be in the Long Trail Saloon at four the next afternoon. He said nothing because he wanted a free hand to do whatever needed to be done. Also, he didn't want to have to worry about looking out for anyone else, should trouble start.

As he approached the two saloons, the Long Trail was on the west side of the street and the Jayhawker was on the east side, and he could see why the Long Trail was the recommended of the two.

The Long Trail Saloon was one of the more substantial-looking buildings in the entire town. It was a real two-story building, as opposed to the false fronts of several of the other buildings along the street. There was a roof over the porch of the building, and the roof acted as a balcony for the second story. Hanging from the roof was a large sign. At the end of the sign was a very good representation of a rider following a trail, which stretched out before the rider, twisting itself into cursive letters to form the saloon's name, The Long Trail. The letters were red, outlined with yellow.

As soon as Falcon pushed through the batwing doors, he stepped to one side, then backed up against the wall as he surveyed the saloon. He wasn't supposed to be met until the next day, but there was a possibility that, like him, someone had come a day early. A quick perusal did not turn up any face that he recognized. He felt safe to move on into the saloon, because he believed he would have recognized Loomis or any of his men. He had a clear memory of them, from having encountered them at the stagecoach way station where they killed the shotgun guard and attempted to steal the money the stage was transporting.

The saloon was filled with its evening trade. At first it seemed a little quieter than normal; then he realized that the ubiquitous sound of piano music was missing. At the rear of the room, an empty beer mug and a half-full ashtray conveniently placed by the piano provided the evidence that, though nobody was playing the piano at the moment, there was a piano player.

Falcon stepped up to the bar and ordered a beer, and when it was served, he turned around to survey the room as he drank it. The bar was crowded and most of the tables were full, but he did not see one person that he recognized.

Four people were sitting at the table nearest the piano — three young cowboys and a bar girl. The table had one empty whiskey bottle and a second that was half-full, indicating that the bar girl was doing a very good job of pushing drinks.

Falcon took a swig of his beer and smiled as he saw the bar girl flirtatiously playing with the ear of one of the cowboys with one hand while, with the other, she was refilling his glass from the bottle on the table.

At one of the other tables, a lively card game was in progress. The table was crowded with stacks of money in coin and paper, as well as empty beer mugs. There were two brass spittoons within easy spitting distance of the players.

"How the hell did you do that? I had a pair of kings showin'. How'd you know I didn't have 'em backed up? You usin' mirrors or somethin'?" one of the cardplayers asked, obviously agitated by the hand just played.

"Now, just hold on here. You're not accusin' me of cheatin', are you, Hayes?" one of the other players asked. "Because I don't think I would like that very much."

"No," Hayes said, holding his hand up as if to deny the suggestion. "I ain't said you was cheatin', or nothin' like that. I'm just wonderin' how you can do that, is all."

The slender, well-dressed man began pulling a pile of money toward him from the middle of the table. He chuckled in satisfaction as he did so.

"I did it, Hayes, because I am a professional gambler and I know that, despite what the average cowpoke believes, poker is not about luck."

"What do you mean, it ain't about luck? You gotta have the cards," Hayes said.

"Oh, yes, you have to have the cards, but if you are in a game with three other players, the odds are that each of the four will get winning cards twenty-five percent of the time. Something has to change that balance so that one person wins more than the others. That something is skill. I have spent many years developing my skill as a poker player. And one thing I have learned is to tell when someone is trying to run a bluff. No one, absolutely no one, can run a bluff on me. I always say that's what separates the professionals from the amateurs. You,

Hayes, are an amateur. Whereas I am a professional."

Falcon drank his beer and watched as the gambler continued to hold court.

"Look at it this way, young man. When you play with J. T. Finley, you can plan to lose more than you win. On the other hand, you could regard it as going to school to learn just how to play the game. You are paying for an education."

"You're full of shit," Hayes said.

"Are you ready for another lesson?" Finley asked he shuffled the cards for another deal.

"Deal me out," Hayes said, getting up from the table.

Finley turned toward Falcon.

"Sir, I see you have been watching us. As you can see, there is now a chair open. Would you care to join the game?"

Falcon tossed the rest of his drink down, then wiped the back of his hand across his mouth. He had learned long ago that it was sometimes easier to pick up information through casual conversation over a few drinks and a deck of cards than to ask for it outright. That was justification enough for joining the card game, though in truth, he did enjoy a good game now and then. And it might be fun to send this pompous ass to school.

"Don't mind if I do," he said. He handed his mug to the bartender in a silent request for a refill.

"Finley is the name. J. T. Finley. And you are?"

"MacCallister. Falcon MacCallister," Falcon replied.

Standing at the end of the bar at that moment was a young man whose name was Denny Dunaway. He liked to be called the "Colorado Kid," though in truth, he was the only one who referred to himself that way.

He turned with a start when he heard Falcon identify himself.

Dunaway had never met Falcon MacCallister, but he knew all about him. And he also knew that someday he would meet him in a gunfight, and he would kill him.

Dunaway had no personal beef with Falcon MacCallister. He just wanted the fame that would come from beating him. In fact, Dunaway had even begun writing his own book about it, a penny dreadful like the ones he had seen about Falcon MacCallister. *The Colorado Kid — Duel in the Street,* the title would be. The subtitle would read, *The*

For a moment, Dunaway felt such a surge of excitement that it was all he could do to keep from challenging MacCallister right here and right now. His hands began to shake so badly that he couldn't hold the drink, and he had to put the glass down on the bar in front of him.

Finley looked up at Falcon as he approached the table. "Do you believe that chairs can be unlucky?" Finley asked. "Because if you do, you can switch that chair with one from another table."

"There is no such thing as an unlucky chair," Falcon said. "There are just players who don't know what they are doing."

"Players who don't know what they are doing, huh? My, my, Mr. MacCallister, I do believe you have taken a page from my book," Finley said. "Suppose we just see if you know what you are doing."

"That sounds agreeable," Falcon said as he sat at the table.

"MacCallister," Finley said as he shuffled the cards. "I do believe that is a name of some note in these parts."

"Yes," one of the other players said. "The actors were just through here a few days ago. Andrew and Rosanna MacCallister, I

226

believe they were. Husband and wife."

"Brother and sister," Falcon corrected.

"No, I believe you are wrong, sir," the player said. "I am quite sure they are husband and wife."

"They are brother and sister," Falcon repeated. "As a matter of fact, they are my brother and sister," he added.

"Oh!" the player said. "Oh! Well, dear me, I suppose you would know, wouldn't you?"

"Mr. MacCallister, I hate to ask such an embarrassing question, but do you have enough money to participate in this game?" Finley asked.

"Will this do?" Falcon asked, putting one hundred dollars down on the table.

"Uh, yes," Finley said. "Yes, that will do quite well, thank you. Yes indeed, I think you will make a fine addition to the game, and your money a fine addition to my wallet," he added with a laugh.

Finley reached for the cards, but Falcon put his own hand on the cards.

"I would prefer a new deck, if you don't mind," Falcon said.

"A new deck? All right," Finley said, picking up a fresh box. Using his thumbnail, he broke the seal, then took the cards out. Removing the joker, he spread the deck out on the table, then flipped the cards over expertly, making a little show of it for the others. "Are you satisfied with the cards?" he asked.

"They suit me," Falcon said.

Finley shuffled the cards and the stiff new pasteboards clicked sharply. His hands moved swiftly, folding the cards in and out, until the law of random numbers became the law of the deck. He shoved the cards toward Falcon, who cut them, then pushed them back.

"Gentlemen, the game is five-card draw," Finley said. He looked at Falcon. "Assuming that is all right with our new player."

"Five-card draw is fine."

Falcon could have won with the first hand, but he purposely played it overcautiously, losing ten dollars in the process.

Finley laughed softly as he dragged in the pot.

"Are you sure you want to play this game, Mr. MacCallister?" he asked. "You just folded on a winning hand."

"I am a cautious player," Falcon said.

"Oh, I love cautious players," Finley said. "My only regret, Mr. MacCallister, is that you will lose your money too quickly. And where is the fun in that?"

Once again, Falcon folded on a hand that could have won had he played a bit more aggressively.

By the third hand, Falcon was down sixty-five dollars, but there was forty dollars in the pot, and he had just drawn two cards to complete a diamond flush. He bet ten dollars.

"Wow, ten dollars," Finley teased. "That's a pretty heavy bet. You sure you want to bet that much?"

"Yes, I — I think so," Falcon said hesitantly.

"All right, then, I tell you what. I'll just see your ten, and raise it ten."

"Damn, Finley," one of the other players said. "Mr. MacCallister just sat in to play a friendly game of cards. This ain't no duel. I'm out."

"So am I," the other player said.

"And it isn't a game of checkers either," Finley said. "If this game is too rich for you, you just sit it out until MacCallister and I are finished. Now what are you going to do, Mr. MacCallister? Fold, call, or raise?"

MacCallister made a big show of studying his hand carefully.

"I guess — I guess I'll call," he said hesitantly.

Finley was holding three kings, and he clucked his tongue and shook his head when he saw Falcon's hand.

"You were holding a flush and all you did was call?"

"I thought you might have four kings," MacCallister said. "I didn't want the betting to get out of hand. And as you can see, it was the right move. I won the hand, and I am now twenty-five dollars ahead." MacCallister's smile showed that he was quite proud of himself.

"And you think you are a big winner because you're twenty-five dollars ahead in the game?" Finley laughed, a low, mocking, laugh. "So, should I be worried now?"

"Maybe," Falcon said. "I've been watching you. I think I've about got you figured out."

"You have me figured out, do you?" Finley said.

"Yes, I think so."

"I tell you what, MacCallister, I'm tired of dealing with an amateur. I think I'll just break you this hand. That is, if you are brave enough to stay with me."

"Well, I won't bet good money on bad cards, if that's what you mean," Falcon said.

"You don't want to bet good money on bad cards," Finley repeated. He shook his head. "That sounds like something you would hear at a temperance meeting. God help me, what am I doing in this game? I'm opening with twenty dollars, are you in?"

"Is it all right if I put more money on the table?" Falcon asked.

"Ha! The more money you put on the table, the more I will walk away with," Finley said. "Put all the money you want there."

"I think another one hundred dollars will be enough."

Finley shoved the cards across the table to Falcon. "It's your deal."

When Falcon picked up the cards, he felt of them as he began shuffling, checking for pinpricks and uneven corners, satisfying himself that they were playing with an honest deck.

Falcon dealt the cards. The betting was quite brisk, and within a few moments the pot was over two hundred dollars.

"Now, MacCallister, school's out. It's going to cost you to see what I have," Finley said. "I'm going to bet one hundred dollars."

"Shit, you ain't playin' cards, Finley, you're trying to buy the pot. Damn, I'm out," one of the other players said. The remaining player also dropped out, leaving only Falcon and Finley.

"What about it, mister? It's just you and me now. You want to pay to see what I've got?"

Falcon looked at his cards; then he looked across the table at Finley. A small confident smile spread across his face.

"I'll see your hundred, and raise it a hundred," Falcon said.

"What?" Finley asked in surprise. "What the hell are you holding?"

"Like you say, you are going to have to pay to look at them," Falcon answered. He put the cards down in front of him, four to one side, and one off by itself.

"Son of a bitch, he's got four of a kind," someone said.

"What makes you think that?" said someone else.

"Well, hell, look for yourself. Did you see the way he put them cards down? I tell you, he's got four of a kind."

By now the stakes of the game were high enough to have attracted the attention of everyone else in the saloon, and there were several men standing around the table, watching the game with intense interest. Many had also come to watch in hopes of seeing Finley get beaten, because he had not only won money from nearly everyone in the saloon at one time or another, he had won it with intense arrogance.

"He's bluffin', Finley," one of the other players said. "I got me a gut feelin' that he's bluffin'. Call his hand."

Finley snorted. "You've got a gut feelin', do you, Harry? Well, it's your feelin', but it's my money. I don't see you still in the game."

"Call him," Harry said again.

"You ain't listened to nothin' I've ever told you, have you, Harry?" Finley asked as rubbed his chin and studied Falcon. "You don't play with your gut, you play with your mind. And don't forget, this is the fella who wouldn't even raise a flush."

Falcon smiled across the table at Finley.

"What are you going to do, Finley?" one of the bystanders asked. "Like you told this gentleman a few moments ago, you can't take all night."

"All right, all right, the pot's yours," Finley said, turning his cards up on the table. He had a full house, aces over jacks. "What have you got?"

Falcon looked at his cards, facedown on the table just the way he left them, four in one pile, one in another. He reached out to rake in his pot.

Normally, he would not show his cards if the player hadn't paid to see them. But in this case, part of the pleasure in beating Finley would be in letting Finley see just how he had beaten him.

Smiling, Falcon turned his cards up. He had two jacks and two tens.

"What the hell is this?" Finley gasped, glancing up from the cards with an expression of exasperation on his face. "Are you telling me you beat me with two pairs?"

"He ran a bluff on you, Finley," Harry said. He chuckled. "Ain't you the one, while ago, who said there weren't nobody who could ever beat you with a bluff?"

Those who had gathered to watch the game laughed out loud.

For a moment, Finley's face was clouded with anger; then suddenly, and unexpectedly, he broke out in laughter as well.

"He didn't just run a bluff on me, boys, he set me up!" Finley said. "And it was the smoothest job I ever saw."

Finley stuck his hand out. "Mr. MacCallister," he said. "Day after day I sit here, going on and on about running a school to teach these people how to play cards. But I must confess, sir, you taught me a lesson today. It was well worth the money I lost."

Falcon took Finley's hand and shook it. "You're a good man, Finley. You are all right in my book," MacCallister said.

The others, seeing the building tension melt away, laughed, and breathed a sigh of relief. They knew that this was exactly the kind of thing that could erupt in a killing.

Evidently, there would be no killing here tonight.

CHAPTER EIGHTEEN

Falcon went back to the bar and ordered another beer.

"Where's the best place to put up for the night?" he asked.

"Well, if you're lookin' for company for the night, we've got rooms upstairs," the barkeep said.

"I'm not looking for company."

"In that case, you've got two choices. Ziegenhorn's if you want to sleep cheap. He don't have rooms, but he's got lots of beds upstairs in one big room. You'll probably have to put up with a lot of snorin', though."

"What's the other choice?"

"The Morning Star Hotel. It's just down the street."

"Thanks," Falcon said.

"Draw, MacCallister!" someone shouted.

Instantly, Falcon drew his pistol and turned toward the sound of the voice, seeing a young man reaching for his gun.

However, when that man saw how quickly Falcon had drawn, he changed his mind and let the pistol fall back in the holster as he put his hands up.

"No, no," he said. "Don't shoot, Mr. Mac-Callister! For God's sake, don't shoot!"

"You're the one that invited me to the dance, mister," Falcon said.

"I'm sorry, I'm sorry," the man said. "I thought I could beat you, I . . ." He let the response die on his lips.

"Are you with Tate?"

"What?"

"Loomis Tate," Falcon said angrily. "Are you with Loomis Tate?"

"No, I — I don't know who or what you are talking about."

"If you aren't with Tate, why did you try to kill me?"

"Because I thought I could. I'm the Colorado Kid and I thought — I thought I could beat you."

"You are the what?" Falcon asked.

"The — the Colorado Kid. You've never heard of me, but someday you will."

"What is your name?" Falcon asked.

"I told you, I'm the Colorado —"

"What is your real name?" Falcon asked, interrupting him.

"Dunaway. Denny Dunaway."

Falcon holstered his pistol. "Dunaway, have you ever killed a man?" he asked.

"Yeah, sure. I've killed plenty of men," Dunaway said.

Falcon didn't answer. Instead, he just continued to stare at Dunaway.

"Well, not plenty of men, but some," Dunaway said.

Falcon still said nothing.

"All right, no, I've never killed anyone yet. But I'm fast. I'm very fast."

"I take it that you've never been shot at either," Falcon asked.

"Well, no, but I'm not afraid to stand up to anyone," Dunaway insisted. "I've just never had the chance to do it before now."

Suddenly, and unexpectedly, Falcon drew his pistol and shot. Those who were looking directly at Dunaway saw a mist of blood and little pieces of flesh fly away from his right earlobe.

"Ow!" Dunaway said, slapping his hand to his ear. As he cupped his hand over the ear, blood began to run through his fingers. "What did you do that for?"

"I want you to know what you are letting yourself in for," Falcon said. "When you are facing another man with a gun, death can come quick. In your case, you just lost a part of your ear. It was a cheap lesson."

Dunaway didn't answer. Instead, he just stared at Falcon, all the while trying to hold back the blood from the wound in his ear.

Falcon took one more swallow of his beer, then nodded at the bartender.

"I reckon I'll go check out that hotel you told me about," he said.

"Tell 'em Jake Conroy sent you," the bartender suggested.

"Why? Will it get me a better deal?"

Conroy laughed. "No, but it will get me a dime," he said. "I get a dime ever'time I send someone over."

"I'll do that for you," Falcon replied with a smile.

"MacCallister, wait!" Dunaway shouted just as Falcon reached the door.

Falcon whirled around, but saw that Dunaway had made no move to get to his gun.

Dunaway pointed at him.

"This ain't over," he said.

Falcon nodded, then picking up his saddlebags, turned and left the saloon.

CHAPTER NINETEEN

Kelly Tate had watched the whole thing unfold between Falcon and Dunaway. Kelly was the one who had come into town to meet Falcon, because he was the only one of Loomis's gang that Falcon had never seen.

Kelly had recognized Falcon from the description provided by Loomis and the others. When a big man came in, carrying saddlebags over his shoulders, Kelly was fairly certain he had the right man. Then, he heard MacCallister introduce himself to the others in the card game.

Kelly wasn't supposed to meet him until the following afternoon. He had just come into town ahead of time in order to get the feel of things. He couldn't say that he was all that surprised that MacCallister had come in early as well.

No problem, Kelly still had the advantage. He now knew who MacCallister was. Mac-

Callister didn't know who he was. It gave him a sense of power to be able to observe without being observed. It was like watching a pissant crawl across a rock. Kelly laughed at his analogy. He liked thinking of MacCallister as a pissant.

Kelly felt as if he was well in charge of the situation, until he saw Dunaway challenge MacCallister. That could have changed everything. If Dunaway had killed MacCallister, then the money would have been lost.

He was glad that MacCallister wasn't killed. If anyone was going to kill MacCallister, he was the one who was going to do it.

It wasn't until that moment that the idea of killing MacCallister came into Kelly's mind. There would never be a better opportunity for him to do it. If he killed MacCallister tonight, everyone would think that Dunaway did it.

A broad smile spread across Kelly's face. He would kill MacCallister, then show up back at the way station with the money already in hand. He'd like to see the expressions on their faces then when he . . .

Wait a minute, he thought. Why go back to the way station at all? After all, if he killed MacCallister, wouldn't the money rightly be his? Yes, they would be pissed with him, but they had no right to be. Hell, if he hadn't gotten them out of jail, they would've been hung. They'd all be worm food by now. By damn, this money was rightly his, and they had no right to be pissed at him.

Twenty thousand dollars. What could a man do with twenty thousand dollars?

He could go back East, maybe to someplace like St. Louis or New York or Boston. He didn't know much about any of those places, but he had heard of them. He had heard of something called a Boston Tea Party. He wasn't sure what you did at a tea party, but if he was going to be rich, then he would probably need to go to one.

Kelly saw Dunaway standing down at the end of the bar. Nobody else was around him, and he was staring morosely into his beer. His ear had stopped bleeding, but it was crusty from old blood.

Kelly walked up to him.

"What do you want?" Dunaway asked.

"He cheated you," Kelly said.

"What?"

"Well, when you challenge a man to draw, you expect him to turn around and face you, then draw. I seen what happened. You challenged him to draw, but he pulled his gun first, then turned around. You, bein' a fair man, wasn't expectin' that."

"You're right!" Dunaway said. "I wasn't expectin' it. I mean, by the time he turned, he already had his gun in his hand. What was I to do?"

"You done what any sane man would do," Kelly said. "You kept your gun in your holster."

"Yeah. A lot of good it did me," he said, putting his hand up to his earlobe. "The son of a bitch shot me anyway."

"You know what I think?" Kelly asked.

"What's that?"

"I think if you kilt him now, nobody would blame you for it. I mean, hell, ever'one in here seen him shoot off part of your ear. It would be self-defense, pure and simple."

"Yeah," Dunaway said nervously. "Yeah, I know what you mean. And I'm going to face him down, too, I just need to — uh . . ."

"Why do you need to face him down?" Kelly asked. "Just do it."

"What do you mean, just do it?"

"Just kill the son of a bitch," Kelly said. "Ever'body seen him threaten you, ever'body seen him try to kill you. He missed and hit you in the ear, but make no mistake, he was aimin' to hit you right between the eyes."

"No, I think he was —"

"He was aimin' to hit you right between

243

the eyes," Kelly said, interrupting Dunaway. "Ever'body seen it. That means if you kill him, no matter how you do it, it would be self-defense."

"I'll do it," Dunaway said resolutely. "You want a drink?"

"I don't mind if I do."

"Barkeep, bring a drink for my friend," Dunaway called.

"You said you were going to do it," Kelly said as the bartender brought the drink. "You're going to do what?"

"I'm going to kill MacCallister," Dunaway said.

Kelly lifted the drink to his lips, noticing the bartender's reaction as he did so.

Even as Kelly was talking to Dunaway, he was forming a new plan. Rather than killing MacCallister and blaming it on Dunaway, why not let Dunaway actually do the killing? Kelly could go with him, not only to goad Dunaway into actually doing it, but also to take care of things when it was over.

What Kelly planned to do was to knock Dunaway out after MacCallister was killed. That way he would be able to take the saddlebags without any interference, and he would leave Dunaway there to take the responsibility.

"I'll go with you if you want me to," Kelly said.

"What? Go with me where?"

"Why, to kill MacCallister, of course," Kelly said.

"Why would you want to do that?"

"Because you're my friend," Kelly said. "I wouldn't want to see my friend have to face someone like MacCallister all by yourself. No, sir, when you kill that son of a bitch, I'll be there."

"You will?"

"Absolutely. And I'll tell people how you beat him fair and square," Kelly added. He smiled. "Think of it . . . the Colorado Kid kills Falcon MacCallister in a head-to-head gunfight."

"I thought, uh, I thought you said I wouldn't have to face him."

"You don't have to face him," Kelly said. "I'm just saying what I'll be telling others about it."

"Oh, yeah," Dunaway said. "Yeah, that's good."

Kelly looked at the clock standing on the wall at the back of the saloon. According to the clock it was eleven-fifteen.

"Come on," Kelly said. "I heard him say that he was going to take a room at the Morning Star. This would be as good a time as any to take care of it."

"I guess you're right," Dunaway said a little hesitantly.

"By this time tomorrow, the Colorado Kid will be known all over the West as the man who kilt Falcon MacCallister."

"Yeah," Dunaway said. He finished his drink and wiped the back of his hand across his mouth. "Yeah!" he said more resolutely. "Come on, what are we waiting for?"

The lobby of the Morning Star hotel was only dimly lit by a lantern that was burning very low. They could hear snoring, and knew that it was the night clerk.

Kelly held his finger to his lips; then the two of them walked quietly across the lobby floor to the counter. There, Kelly turned the book around and, moving it into the light of the lamp, looked at the registered guests. He found what he was looking for on the bottom line.

Falcon MacCallister, MacCallister Valley, Col — Room 12

He pointed the entry out to Dunaway; then the two of them started up the stairs to find Room Twelve.

The hallway was long and narrow, flanked

on both sides by numbered doors. Because of the way the numbers were running, Kelly knew that the room they were looking for would be at the far end of the hallway.

The hallway was illuminated by lanterns that were mounted along the wall. Kelly reached up to extinguish the first lantern. Dunaway extinguished the next and, as they progressed down the hall, they were followed by lengthening shadows behind them.

Falcon wasn't sure what woke him up. It may have been a creaky board from someone walking in one of the other rooms, but something had awakened him. He lay in bed, very quietly, trying to hear another sound, but he heard nothing.

Then, a little flash of some kind caused him to look up into the transom window over his door. The transom was open to encourage a cross breeze from his open window. Because of the way the transom was tilted, he could see, in the window's reflection, the glowing lights of the hallway.

And yet, even as he looked, he saw a lamp go out. It wasn't until then that he realized that more than half the hallway was now in darkness. It seemed pretty strange to have the lanterns all burning out at approximately the same time.

Then he saw, in the window's reflection, two men moving up the hallway. He saw one reach up to extinguish a lantern, and he knew that the lights were being purposely extinguished.

But why?

As the two men moved closer to his room, he no longer had to ask why the lights were being put out. He recognized one of the men as Denny Dunaway, the young man with whom he had had a confrontation in the bar. Both Dunaway and the man with him had their pistols drawn and they were coming quietly, but determinedly, toward his room.

Sliding his pistol out of the holster that hung from the bedpost, he stepped quickly to one side of the room and waited.

Looking back at his bed, he could see quite clearly that nobody was in bed.

Moving quickly, Falcon stepped back over to his bed, fluffed up the pillow and the covers, then returned to his position on the side of the room.

As the men got closer, the angle of the transom window was such that it no longer showed their position, so he lost the advantage of being able to watch as they approached.

He waited.

Suddenly his door burst open, having been kicked in by the two men who were outside.

"Draw, MacCallister!" Dunaway shouted. He began shooting at the bed, the muzzle flashes of his pistol filling the room with light as the crashes of gunfire filled it with noise.

"Dunaway! I'm over here!" Falcon shouted.

"What?" Dunaway replied. "What the hell?"

Dunaway whirled toward Falcon and fired.

Falcon had to give the young man credit. His reaction was much faster than Falcon had expected it would be, no doubt because he was already committed to what he was doing.

Dunaway's bullet burned by Falcon's head, just missing returning the favor of a mangled ear. The bullet plunged into the wall beside Falcon with a thocking sound, just as Falcon returned fire.

Dunaway had fired a total of five rounds before Falcon even fired. Falcon fired only once, but he needed only one shot. Dunaway fell out into the hallway floor.

"Dunaway!" Kelly shouted.

It wasn't until then that Falcon remembered that he had seen two men in the hall.

That meant there was another one out there after him.

Falcon moved quickly to the door to be able to confront the other man, but he had already run to the far end of the hall, disappearing into the darkness. Falcon started after him, but couldn't fire because he couldn't see and was afraid someone innocent might open the door to their room, just to see what all the noise was about.

From the far end of the hallway, Falcon heard a crash of glass. The son of a bitch had leaped through the window to escape!

CHAPTER TWENTY

Answering Marshal Kingsley's request that he do so, Falcon MacCallister showed up in Judge T. Bonley Craig's office the next morning. Craig's office was in the back of the town courthouse, and he stepped out of his office when Falcon and Kingsley arrived.

"Good morning, gentlemen," Judge Craig said. "I hear we had a little excitement last night."

Craig was a tall, gaunt, white-haired man in his late seventies. He had been a colonel during the Civil War, assigned to the Judge Advocate Corps.

"That's right, Your Honor," Kingsley said.

"And this is the man who was involved in the shooting?" Craig nodded toward Falcon.

"Yes, sir."

"Well, there must be a pretty strong case of justifiable homicide; otherwise, you would have him in jail."

"Your Honor, if you would allow me, I

would like to give you the results of my investigation," Kingsley said.

"By all means, please do so, Marshal," Craig said.

"Wait out here, would you, Mr. MacCallister, until I speak with the judge?" Kingsley said.

"I'll wait."

"Mr. MacCallister, I trust you will still be here when the marshal finishes his report," Craig said. "But just to make it official, I hereby bind you with a court order to wait right here until I release you."

"I'll be right here when you come out," Falcon said.

As Falcon waited, he studied a Currier and Ives lithograph titled: "American Express Trains, Leaving the Junction." It was a painting of two trains, running together on parallel tracks, with their bell-shaped stacks sending smoke billowing up into the night. There was a cloud cover in the sky, but a hole in the clouds allowed a full moon to peek through, limning the clouds in luminescent silver. Huge gas lamps glowed just in front of the stacks, while every window of every passenger car was bright with light.

It was a pleasant picture to contemplate, and Falcon could easily understand why the judge had it on his wall.

The door to Judge Craig's inner office opened, and he and Kingsley stepped out.

"Still here, I see, Mr. MacCallister?" Judge Craig said, his voice jovial.

"Yes, sir. I'm still here," Falcon answered. He smiled. "I'm not about to violate a court order."

"Well, it's good to see that you are a man of your word," Craig said.

"My pa used to say that a man's worth had nothing to do with how much money he had. A man's worth was measured by things like integrity, loyalty, courage, honor, and his word."

"I met your father once, during the war," Judge Craig said. "Yes, sir, Jamie Ian MacCallister was a man who could be measured by every one of those qualities."

"I believe he was, sir."

"Now, about this ruckus in the hotel last night," Judge Craig said, stroking his jaw with a long, thin hand that was spotted and wrinkled with age. "Marshal Kingsley has done a thorough investigation of the case. There were several witnesseses in the Long Trail who said they would testify that they saw the decedent challenge you last night. They said that you could have killed him then, and had every right to do so, but you spared his life. And the bartender will testify that later, after you had already left the saloon, he heard Dunaway say he was going to kill you.

"And if that wasn't enough, there are five empty cartridges in Dunaway's gun, and there are four bullet holes in the pillow on the bed, and one in the wall. He was shot one time, and when the marshal examined your gun, he found only one empty cartridge. Is that about right?"

"Yes, sir," Falcon replied.

"Do you have anything to add?"

"Yes, sir."

Craig looked at Kingsley, surprised to hear that Falcon had something to add. Kingsley lifted his shoulders as if saying he had no idea what Falcon was about to say.

"All right then, let's hear it," Judge Craig said.

"There was someone else out in the hall last night," Falcon said. "Someone was with Dunaway."

"Oh, yes, Kingsley did mention that," Craig said. "Did you get a look at him?"

"No, I did not. I think that, as part of their plan to attack me, the two men extinguished all the lamps out in the hall, and by the time I got to the door, the second assailant, whoever he was, was already back into the dark end of the hall."

"What about before, in the saloon? Was Dunaway with anyone that you could tell?" Craig asked.

Falcon shook his head. "As far as I could tell, he was alone."

"All right," Judge Craig said. "Marshal, I congratulate you on a very thorough investigation. I don't believe there is any need to hold an official inquiry. That is, unless you have other evidence to report."

"I've given you everything I have, Your Honor."

"Then, in the matter of the death of Denny Dunaway, I rule it justifiable homicide and will have a court document drawn up declaring same. Mr. MacCallister, the court order requiring you to remain here is lifted. You are free to go."

"Thank you, Your Honor," Falcon said.

When Judge Craig extended his hand, Falcon shook it. Then, Falcon extended his hand to Marshal Kingsley.

"Thank you, Marshal, for, as the judge said, a most thorough investigation."

"I was glad to be of service to you, Mr. MacCallister. I just wish I had some idea as to who the other man was. It could be dangerous not knowing. He could try again."

"I'll just have to be vigilant," Falcon said.

"Ha! As if you weren't all the time," Kingsley replied.

Falcon reached for his saddlebags, then slung them across his shoulder.

"Marshal, this has taken up most of the morning. It's nearly noon now. How about letting me buy you lunch?" Falcon asked.

Kingsley smiled. "I never turn down the opportunity for a free lunch," he said. He pointed to the saddlebags. "You've been carrying those things ever since I saw you. Would you like me to lock them up in my office for you?"

"No, thanks, they're no trouble. I can keep up with them," Falcon said without elaboration. "Now, about lunch, do you have a suggestion as to where we might eat?"

"Ziegenhorn's?" Kingsley suggested.

Falcon smiled painfully. "Uh, no offense, Ziegenhorn is a nice fellow, but I've eaten at Ziegenhorn's. Is there any other place you might suggest?"

"Well, we could go to Tinkers' Café I supposed. He charges a little more than Ziegenhorn."

"Is his food better?"

"Oh, yes, it's about as good a place as any in town," Kingsley said.

"I don't mind paying a little extra if the quality is there," Falcon said.

Tinkers' Café was at the far end of town from the courthouse, and as they passed by the newspaper office, Blanton came running out.

"Mr. MacCallister, would you grant me an interview about the events of last night?" Blanton asked.

"We're just going to lunch, Tom," Kingsley said.

"No problem. I'll just lock up and come to lunch with you, if you don't mind."

"Uh, I'm not sure," Kingsley began, but Falcon interrupted him.

"I've offered to buy him lunch and he's not sure how far the invitation goes," Falcon said to Blanton. "I had a good night at the card table last night, so come along."

"Yes, I heard you taught Mr. J. T. Finley a lesson in how to run a bluff," Blanton said, chuckling. "Just let me lock up."

Falcon and Kingsley waited until the newspaper editor locked his office; then the three of them continued on down the street until they reached Tinkers' Café.

Tinkers' Café was a small, white building with two large windows in front. Even before they reached it, they could smell the delicious aromas of today's fare.

They found a table at the back of the room, and when Falcon took the chair that put his back to the wall, neither of the other men challenged him.

They were halfway through their meal when Falcon saw him. He was tall and slim, and wearing an oversized handlebar mustache. Falcon had seen him the night before, in the saloon. Only, when he saw him last night, there was no scar on his forehead.

"That man," Falcon said.

"What man?" Kingsley asked, his mouth full of chicken and dumplings.

Falcon nodded toward the man who had just come in.

"That man over there. He has a scar on his forehead."

Kingsley chuckled. "Is that what we're doing now? Because whoever was with Dunaway jumped out the window, we should be looking for men with scars?"

"Fresh scars," Falcon replied. "When I saw him in the saloon last night, he had no scars. Now he has a long, red slash on his forehead. And if we got a closer look at him, I expect he might have scars in other places as well."

"Well, I can't just go up to people and ask them to let me look for scars," Kingsley said. He was twisting around in his seat as he spoke. "On the other hand, if you think he is . . . what the hell?" Kingsley said, interrupting his statement right in the middle.

"Crack, that's one of the . . ." Blanton started, but Kingsley answered before the editor could finish.

"Yes, he *is* one of them," Kingsley said.

"One of them?" Falcon asked. "One of who?"

"One of the men who came by the store the day before your brother and sister were taken from the train. He was with Loomis Tate and the albino."

"Are you sure?" Falcon asked.

"Yes, we're sure," Blanton said, answering for both of them.

"I thought you knew Loomis Tate and all his men," Kingsley said.

"I know them all except for Loomis's brother Kelly. And if that man was one of them, as you say, then I would take bets that he is Kelly Tate."

"And you say you saw him last night?" Kingsley asked.

"Yes."

"I wonder what he's doing in town. You'd think he'd be as far away from here as he can get."

"He's here to see me, I expect," Falcon said.

"See you for what?"

"We were supposed to meet in the Long

259

Trail this afternoon. He's here to give me directions on how I am to pay the twenty thousand dollars."

"Twenty thousand dollars?" Kingsley said, nearly choking on his food. "What twenty thousand dollars?"

"The twenty thousand dollars I am supposed to pay to ransom my brother and sister."

"My God, man! Do you actually have that kind of money?" Blanton asked.

"Yeah," Falcon said. He patted the saddlebags. "I've got the money."

Kingsley laughed out loud. "I'll be damned. So that's why you've been keeping those saddlebags with you night and day. That's where you are keeping the money, isn't it?"

"Yes."

Kingsley wiped his lips with his napkin, then pushed back from the table. "I think I'll just ask Mr. Tate where he was last night."

"Don't spook him too much," Falcon said. "I'm going to need him to be able to find Andrew and Rosanna."

"I'm just going to ask him a few questions," Kingsley said. He started toward Kelly. "Mr. Tate, I wonder if I could ask you where you were last night?"

Suddenly, and without warning, Kelly Tate pulled his pistol.

"Eeeeeek!" a woman screamed.

"He's got a pistol!" a man shouted.

"Put that away, Tate, I just want to . . ." Kingsley began, but that was as far as he got.

Kelly pulled the trigger and the gun boomed loudly, sending out a billowing cloud of gun smoke. The impact of the bullet drove Kingsley back.

"Uhnn!" Kingsley said, grabbing his chest with both hands. He took a couple of staggering steps before he collapsed.

"Damn!" Falcon shouted. He was swearing at himself for allowing Kingsley to confront Tate in the first place.

Falcon had not anticipated anything like this, so he had not drawn his pistol. And now, because he was sitting down at the table, he was at a disadvantage. Kelly Tate realized that, and he swung his pistol toward the table where Falcon and Blanton were still sitting.

Blanton's mouth and eyes were open in shock over what he had just witnessed, and he was just sitting there unable to move. Falcon lost time in going for his own gun, because his first inclination was to get the newspaper editor out of the line of fire. He did that by sweeping his arm out, knocking Blanton's chair over so that the newspaper editor wound up on the floor.

That gave Kelly the opportunity to get a shot off. Kelly fired and the bullet hit the water pitcher on Falcon's table, shattering the pitcher and sending the water and tiny shards of glass flying about.

Kelly pulled the hammer back to shoot a third time, but he never got this shot off. By now Falcon had drawn his own pistol and he raised it up, cocking it even as he was bringing it up, and pulling the trigger as he brought the gun to bear.

Unlike Kelly, who had wasted his chance, Falcon's shot was unerringly accurate. Because Falcon was sitting and Kelly was standing, Falcon's bullet went in just under Kelly's chin, then burst out through the top of his head. Kelly fell backward onto a dining table still occupied by a man and a woman who had not had time to react to the speed of events.

Falcon put his pistol back in his holster and hurried over to see to Crack Kingsley. Blanton got there nearly as quickly.

Kingsley's breathing was coming in labored gasps, and as he breathed, little flecks of blood appeared on his lips. The bullet had penetrated his lungs.

"Oh," Kingsley said. "Oh, this is bad, isn't it?"

"Get the doctor!" Blanton shouted. "Someone, please, get the doctor!"

"No need in getting ole Doc Walton away from his lunch," Kingsley said. He tried to laugh, but his laughter turned into a little coughing spell, which just brought up more blood. "We both know I won't live until he gets here."

"Crack, oh, Crack," Blanton said. He reached down to grab his friend's hand.

"You know," Kingsley said. "I'm about to die, but I'm not afraid. I mean, one hundred years from now, everyone in here will be dead. I'm just not afraid. It's sort of funny when you think about it. You spend your whole life afraid of dying, then, when it actually happens, you figure it's not that big of a thing after all."

"You are a courageous man, Marshal Kingsley," Falcon said. "I should not have let you confront him."

"It was my job. Do you think he was the other man last night?"

"I'm sure he was."

"Did you kill him?"

"Yes."

"I thought you wanted to talk to him, to find out about your brother and sister."

263

"I did."

"But you killed him."

"I had no other choice," Falcon said.

"How will you find your brother and sister now?"

"I'll find them," Falcon said.

A faint smile crossed Kingsley's lips. "You know what?" he said. "I think that you will find them. And I think everything is going to turn out right for you."

"Does it hurt, Crack?" Blanton asked.

"No," Kingsley answered. "No, that's the funny thing. It doesn't hurt at . . ."

Kingsley stopped in mid-sentence, his labored breathing halted, and his eyes, still open, began to glaze over.

CHAPTER TWENTY-ONE

Loomis, Strayhorn, Logan, and the albino were out by the corral. All but Logan were saddling their horses.

"Why do I have to stay?" Logan asked.

"I'll explain it to you again," Loomis replied. "Kelly is going to bring MacCallister to the North Fork, where MacCallister will think that we are holding his brother and sister for him. Instead, we will ambush him there."

"What about the money?"

"After we kill him, we'll get the money, come back here to split it, then each of us go our own way."

"What about them?" Logan asked, nodding back toward the house.

"What do you mean, what about them? I thought we had already agreed that we were going to kill them."

"Yeah, that's just my point," Logan said. "If we're goin' to kill them anyway, why not just do it now and be done with it? That way we can all be together when we take the money from MacCallister."

"Huh-uh," Loomis said. "Those two are our insurance."

"Insurance?"

"Yes, just in case something goes wrong."

"What could go wrong? You said you had it all figured out."

"There's always something that can go wrong," Loomis said. "Only a fool doesn't plan for it."

"How do I . . ." Logan began, then he stopped.

"How do you what?"

"How do I know you will actually come back here? You know, if the money is there and all, I don't have any — what was the word you used? Insurance? I don't have any insurance that you will come back and I'll get my share."

"Insurance? We don't need insurance among ourselves," Loomis said with a little chuckle. "All we need is a little trust."

"Trust," Logan repeated. "You mean the only insurance I have is trust that you will come back?"

"That's all the insurance you need."

"You said only a fool doesn't make plans in case something goes wrong."

"Oh for chrissake, Logan, I'll stay," the albino said. He had been saddling his horse, but now he took the saddle off and carried it back into the barn.

"You don't have to do that," Logan said. "I was just . . ."

"I know what you were just," the albino said. "You were just moanin' and belly-achin'. Well, I'm tired of listenin' to it. Saddle your horse and go with them."

Logan grinned broadly. "All right!" he said. Then, he added cautiously, "That is, if you are sure you don't mind."

"I don't mind, and I'm not worried about getting my share," the albino said.

"See there, Logan?" Loomis said. "The albino knows the meaning of trust."

The albino pulled his pistol, then rotated the cylinder as if checking the load in all the chambers.

"Yeah, trust," he said, as he held up his pistol, "and a loaded forty-four. If I don't get my share of the money, I will hunt each one of you down and kill each and every one of you."

The albino tried to ameliorate his comment with a smile. But his pasty-white face gave a macabre aspect to the smile that negated any humor in it.

"You'll get your share," Loomis promised.

"I know I will," the albino replied.

The frozen smile on the albino's face reminded Logan of the perpetual smile on a skull, and he shivered involuntarily.

"Let's go," Loomis said.

The albino walked up to the porch of the house, but remained outside until the others rode off. Then, with the drum of hoofbeats still audible, he opened the door and stepped back inside. Andrew and Rosanna were sitting side by side, tied in chairs.

"Well now, children," the albino said. "It looks like it's just you and me."

"Why?" Andrew asked. "Where did the others go?"

"They went to get the money."

"What money?"

"The money your brother is going to pay to get you back."

"You mean Falcon knows that you have us?" Andrew asked.

"Of course he knows. Loomis sent him a note. How else would we get the money if we didn't tell him?"

Andrew smiled. "That's where you boys made your first mistake," he said.

"What was our first mistake?"

"Telling Falcon that you had us. Don't you know that he will come for us?"

"We're countin' on him comin' for you.

And we're countin' on him to bring the money." The albino chuckled. "Only, when he shows up with the money, well, let's just say that things won't be goin' the way he plans."

Andrew shook his head. "On the contrary. Knowing my brother as I do, I believe that things will go exactly as he plans."

"However it goes, it won't make no difference to the two of you," the albino said. "You're our prisoners, and you're going to stay our prisoners until we decide what to do with you."

"In the meantime, can you loosen the ropes?" Rosanna asked. "They are so tight that they are cutting off the circulation to my hands."

"Sure, I'll loosen the ropes," the albino said. He walked over to Rosanna's chair and untied the ropes that held her hands behind the chair. Then he untied her feet and legs, completely freeing her. "You want to stand up and walk around a bit? Maybe get some circulation back?"

"Yes," Rosanna said. "Oh, yes. Thank you. What about my brother?"

"What about him?"

"Are you going to untie him as well?"

"I don't think so."

"Please," Rosanna said. "Don't you see? If

you don't untie him as well, then I don't want to be untied either."

The albino laughed. "It don't make no difference what you want, girlie. It's your job to keep me happy; it is not *my* job to keep *you* happy," he said. "Now, get up and walk around, get some feelin' back in them arms and legs."

"But . . ."

"Do it, Rosanna," Andrew ordered.

"Andrew, I can't with you —"

"Do it!" Andrew said again.

Nodding, Rosanna stood up, rubbed her wrists a few times, then walked around.

"I tell you what, girlie," the albino said. "While you're a'walkin' aroun' like that, how 'bout takin' off them clothes?"

"What?" Rosanna gasped. "Are you telling me to get undressed?"

"Yeah, sort of," the albino said. "What I actual want you to do is just start takin' 'em off real slowlike. You know, your shoes, your stockings, just one thing at a time."

"I will not do it," Rosanna said adamantly.

"I'll kill you if you don't," the albino said. He pointed his gun at her and cocked it.

"You're probably going to kill us anyway," Rosanna said. "So go ahead."

Rosanna's answer surprised the albino, and his surprise showed in his face.

"Are you tellin' me you don't care if I kill you or not?" he asked.

"That's exactly what I'm telling you," Rosanna said. "If you are going to shoot me, shoot, you maggot-faced pig."

Inasmuch as his features could show expression, the albino flashed anger. Then, inexplicably, he smiled.

"All right," he said. "You've shown me how brave you are with your own life. What about your brother?" The albino pointed his pistol at Andrew. "Now, you start takin' off them clothes, girlie, or I'll shoot him."

"No, don't!" Rosanna said.

The albino smiled. "You goin' to start takin' 'em off?"

"Rosanna, you don't have to do anything you don't want to," Andrew said.

"Oh, yes, she does, boy," the albino said. " 'Cause if she don't, I'm goin' to splatter your brains all over the place."

"I'll do it, I'll do it," Rosanna said.

"That's a good girl. Do it real slow now," the albino said.

As the albino was looking at Rosanna, he didn't see the slight head movement Andrew made. He didn't see it, but Rosanna did. Andrew was telling her to move a bit to her left.

Rosanna knew, immediately, what Andrew

271

wanted. He wanted her to position the albino in a way that would prevent him from having any peripheral vision of her brother. She had no idea what Andrew had in mind, but whatever it was, she would help in any way she could. And for now, that meant she was going to have to keep the albino's eyes glued to her.

Rosanna moved to a chair, then lifted one foot up onto the chair. As she did so, she let her skirt fall back, disclosing a long, well-shaped leg, partially concealed by the pantaloons she was wearing.

"You know," she said in a throaty voice. "When I did this for King Leopold II of Belgium, I had music playing."

"You took off your clothes for a king?" the albino said.

Leaning over in such a way as to show some cleavage, Rosanna began unbuckling her shoes.

"Oh, yes," she said. "What could I do? He was royalty. I'm just a helpless woman."

"Did you — did you take off all your clothes?" the albino asked, his voice thick.

Behind the albino, Rosanna could see that, somehow, Andrew had managed to get both his hands untied. Now he was bent forward, untying his feet.

"I got completely naked," Rosanna said.

"He was very complimentary about my —
breasts."

She set the word "breasts" apart from the
rest of the sentence, and as she said the
word, she put her hands under her breasts,
forcing them up to exaggerate the cleavage.

"What do you think?" she asked. "Do you
like my breasts?"

"Don't worry 'bout takin' off your clothes
real slow," the albino said. "I want you to
shuck out of 'em fast."

Rosanna saw Andrew stand up.

"Do you want me to start here?" Rosanna
asked, pulling the top of her dress down
slightly to expose more of her breasts. "Or
do you want me to start here?" she asked,
pulling her skirt up.

"I want you to —"

"I don't like it when you look at my sister
like that," Andrew said in a quiet, calm
voice.

"Well, it don't matter much what you like,
boy. I'm goin' to do whatever —" He began
turning toward Andrew.

The albino was startled to see Andrew
standing less than an arm's length behind
him. Andrew was smiling at him. He was
also holding a chair.

"How did you —" the albino said, but that
was as far as he got. Andrew swung the chair

273

like a baseball bat. He broke the chair alongside Michaels's head, and the albino went down.

"Bravo!" Rosanna said. "Is he dead?"

"No, I don't think so," Andrew said. Kneeling beside the albino, Andrew felt his neck. "He still has a pulse," he said. Andrew unbuckled the albino's gunbelt, then put it on.

"How did you get loose?"

"I've been working on it all morning," Andrew said. He chuckled. "When you asked him to loosen my wrists too, I winced. That would have given it away."

"Oh, I'm sorry."

"Don't be sorry. You held his attention long enough to let me finish. Come on, let's get out of here."

"Do you have any idea where to go?"

"I don't think it matters," Andrew said. "Anywhere we go is going to be better than here."

"What about him?" Rosanna pointed to the albino's prostrate figure.

"I should kill him," Andrew said. Pulling the pistol from its holster, he pointed it at the albino, then cocked it.

"Andrew, are you . . . ?"

"Sure that I want to do this?" Andrew said, finishing the question. He sighed. "No,

I'm not sure." He let the hammer down slowly on the pistol, then returned it to the holster. "In fact, I can't do it."

The albino came to while they were talking, but Andrew hit him again, this time with the butt of his own pistol, and Michaels went out again.

Ten minutes later, they had two horses saddled.

"Let's go," Andrew said.

"Which way?"

"That way," Andrew said, pointing south.

"Let's go that way," Rosanna said, pointing north.

"Why north?"

"Look at their tracks," Rosanna said, pointing to the tracks of three horses. "They went south."

"Well, if you knew which way we should go, why did you ask me in the first place?"

"To make you feel good," Rosanna answered with a little laugh. She urged her horse into a gallop, heading north, and Andrew followed.

They left the way station at a gallop, and held it for well over a mile before slowing to a trot, then to a walk.

"Let's give the horses a rest," Andrew said. "We're going to have to depend on them for a while. It won't be good to run them into the ground."

"I agree," Rosanna said. She leaned forward, patted her horse on the neck, and laughed.

"What is it? What are you laughing about?"

"I was just thinking," she said. "After this, you won't have to be making up stories about your past. You are living out exactly what you say you are."

"After this?" Andrew asked.

"Yes."

Andrew laughed as well. "That's what I like about you, Rosanna. You have a lot of confidence."

"Confidence?"

"Yes, confidence. Think about it. You said 'after this' as if you truly believe there will be an after this."

"Oh, I believe it, all right," Rosanna said. "I truly believe that someday we'll be sitting around a table at the Metropole, telling the tale of this great adventure."

"You think so?"

"Oh, I know so. And you'll have everyone in the cast, especially the ladies, hanging on your every word. Why, you'll be their hero," Rosanna teased.

"Oh, I won't be the only center of attention," Andrew said. "What about you?"

"Me? What did I do?"

"Your dance of the seven veils?" Andrew teased. "All the men will be wanting to hear about that in its most minute detail."

"And you will tell it, dear brother?"

"I will."

"And will you do it justice?"

"Justice?"

"Yes. Will you describe it in the seductive manner in which it was performed?" Rosanna asked.

Andrew laughed out loud. "I'll be damned," he said. "I believe you enjoyed that. The next thing you know, you will be wanting to incorporate such a dance into our act."

"And why not? Don't you think such an act would go over well for our audience?" Rosanna asked. "Certainly our audiences are more sophisticated than that albino character."

"A Jezebel," Andrew said, shaking his head. "My sister has turned into a Jezebel." He started his horse forward. "Come on, the horses are rested enough. We need to keep moving."

"Wait," Rosanna said.

"Wait? Wait for what?"

Rosanna tore a little strip of cloth from the hem of her dress and tied it to the branch of a willow tree.

"What is that for?"

"Falcon will be looking for us," she said.

"So will the bad men. What if they see that?"

"I think it's a chance we need to take," Rosanna said.

Andrew thought for a second, then nodded. "You're right," he said.

CHAPTER TWENTY-TWO

The Landers farm sat on top of a gently rising hill. It consisted of a house, barn, smokehouse, and corral. The house itself was surrounded by a white picket fence, and flowers grew in colorful profusion on both sides of a brick sidewalk that ran from the porch of the house down to the gate.

Two women were working in the flower garden, but as Falcon drew closer, he saw that one of the women was actually a girl of about sixteen or so. He stopped outside the gate and called out to them.

"Is this the Landers place?"

The two looked up at him, and the younger one wiped her face with the back of her hand. It left a little smear of dirt on her cheek.

"What do you want, mister?" a man's voice called from the loft of the barn.

Falcon had already seen the man in the barn, and he knew that the man had seen him. He knew also that by the time he reached the house the man was holding a rifle on him.

"Mr. Landers, my name is Falcon Mac-Callister," Falcon said.

"Really?" a young male voice called from the door of the barn. "Are you really Falcon MacCallister?"

The boy came out of the barn. Like his father, the boy had been holding a rifle, but he was no longer pointing it at Falcon. Instead, he was holding it down by his side.

"Jesse!" Landers called. "Jesse, you get back in here! You know better than to expose yourself like that!"

"But Pa, this is Falcon MacCallister!" Jesse said. "Ain't you never heard of him?"

"You are Jesse?" Falcon asked.

"Yes, sir."

"You're the one I came to see."

"Really? You came to see me?"

"What do you want with my boy?" Landers yelled. By now Landers had completely exposed himself and, like the boy, was holding his rifle down by his side.

"I want to talk to him, that's all," Falcon said. "That is, if you don't mind," Falcon said.

"What do you want to talk to my boy about?"

"About Johnny," Falcon said. "I'm after the men who killed your son."

"Just a minute," Landers called back. "Wait right there until I come down."

Falcon waited until Landers came down from the loft and out of the barn. Landers started toward him, still carrying his rifle; then, as if thinking about it, he went back and leaned his rifle against the front of the barn.

Falcon swung down from his horse, and was standing there as Landers approached. Landers brushed his hands together, then extended his right hand.

"I'm Josh Landers," he said.

"Falcon MacCallister," Falcon repeated.

"Wow," the boy said. "I'm Jesse, Mr. Mac-Callister." He extended his hand as well, and Falcon shook it.

"Mr. MacCallister, your name evidently means something to my boy," Landers said. "But I'll be honest with you. I've never heard of you."

"Pop, you know all those books Johnny reads — uh —" Jesse stopped, then corrected himself. "I mean, the ones he used to read?"

"Yes."

"Well, most of 'em is about Falcon Mac-Callister. He's a real famous gunfighter, but he only uses his guns for truth and justice."

"Truth and justice, huh?" Landers replied with a little chuckle.

"Yes, sir, that's what it says on the covers of all the books they've ever wrote about him. They say, 'Falcon MacCallister is a warrior of the plains fighting for truth and justice.' "

"Well, in that case, we can't send him away, can we?" Landers said.

"You know what else? He always says, 'Get ready to eat supper in hell,' just before he kills someone. Don't you, Mr. MacCallister?"

"That's what the books say," Falcon replied. That one phrase had become such a standard part of all the novels about him that, though it wasn't true, he no longer denied it.

"You've killed a lot of people, have you, Mr. MacCallister?" Landers asked.

"Mr. Landers, those are dime novels," Falcon said. "They don't call them 'penny dreadfuls' for nothing."

Landers was silent for a moment; then he chuckled. "Well, I don't suppose I can hold you responsible for what they write about you in those books. You're going after the men who killed Johnny, are you?"

"I am."

"Why? Has someone put up a reward?"

"I don't know," Falcon admitted. "But if nobody has, they should."

"So you're not going after them just for the reward?"

"No."

"So, you are going after them in pursuit of — what is it it says on the cover of all your books? Truth and justice?"

"Well, now, while that is certainly a noble goal," Falcon answered, "the fact is, I'm going after them because they have my brother and sister. They have taken them prisoner."

"I see," Landers said. He nodded. "I admire your honesty, Mr. MacCallister. How about staying for lunch?"

Falcon started to decline the invitation, feeling that he really should be getting on. But he realized that he was hungry, and the idea of a home-cooked meal, as balanced against trail jerky, sounded very good to him.

"All right," he agreed. "Thanks, I will stay for lunch."

The Landers family consisted of Josh and his wife, Mary, their sixteen-year-old daughter, Sue, and thirteen-year-old son, Jesse.

"And, of course, we had Johnny as well," Mary said. "In fact, you are sitting in his chair now." They were all seated around the dinner table.

"Oh, I'm sorry."

"Don't be foolish, you have no cause to be sorry, and I had no cause to say such a thing. It's just that we still miss him," Mary said.

"Of course you do. I've lost people of my own," Falcon said. "I understand the hurt."

"Would you like some potatoes, Mr. Mac-Callister?" Sue asked.

Mary was a good-looking woman and her daughter Sue was already exceptionally pretty. Sitting down to dinner with a family like this made MacCallister realize what had been taken from him when his wife was killed.

"What sort of men would kill a boy over a couple of horses?" Mary asked. Just forming the question brought back bitter memories, and she had to wipe tears from her eyes.

"They are evil personified, Mrs. Landers," Falcon said. "Back in Colorado, they murdered an entire family just to steal some horses."

Falcon went on to explain that they had all been tried and convicted for murder, and were awaiting the hangman's noose when they managed to break out of jail.

"To my sure and certain knowledge they

have killed, to date, six people," Falcon said. He paused for a moment before he continued. "I just hope it isn't two more."

"Two more?" Mary said. Then, realizing that Falcon was talking about his brother and sister, she nodded. "Oh, oh, yes, I see what you are talking about. I pray that they are still safe."

"I thank you for that, Mrs. Landers, especially in light of what you have gone through."

"I hope you kill them," Jesse said. "I hope you kill them all."

"I intend to do just that," Falcon replied.

"Mr. MacCallister, you will excuse me for asking, but why would they have taken your brother and sister?" Mary asked.

"My brother and sister are performers upon the stage in New York," Falcon replied. "They are quite well known, not only in New York but all over the world. Loomis and his bunch took them to hold for ransom."

"I do hope you get to them in time," Landers said. "Now, you said you wanted to talk to Jesse. Be my guest. Jesse, tell him anything he wants to know."

"All right, Pa," Jesse replied.

"First of all, Jesse, I read in the paper that you lay on your back, on the bottom of the

285

pond, breathing through a hollow reed. Is that true?"

"Yes, sir," Jesse replied. "It's the way I used to hide from Johnny."

"Well, let me tell you that I think that is one of the smartest things I've ever heard of," Falcon said. "I congratulate you."

"Maybe it will show up in one of your books someday," Jesse suggested.

Falcon chuckled. "Maybe it will," he agreed. "Now, did you see which way they went when they left?"

"I didn't see them leave 'cause I was still hiding," Jesse said. "But when I come up from the water I saw the tracks, and they was leadin' that way." Jesse pointed.

"North," Landers said.

"Any towns up that way?"

"Not till you get to Gem. And that's a good thirty miles."

"I doubt they would take them into a town. Anything else up there, old mine shafts, line shacks?"

"Nothing that I know of," Landers said. "Though I'm reasonably certain there must be some farms or ranches."

"Pretty has a tie-bar shoe," Sue said.

"Pretty?"

"My horse," Sue said. "It's the horse Jesse was riding that day, one of the horses the men stole. Her name is Pretty, and she has a tie-bar shoe."

"Pretty," Jesse said sneeringly. "Have you ever heard such a dumb name for a horse?"

"Papa said I could name her anything I wanted," Sue said. "And she is so pretty that I named her Pretty."

"And she has a tie-bar shoe, you say?"

"Left forefoot," Landers said. "She has a weak foot, and that seems to help her."

"I thought maybe, that is — if you are going to be tracking them, that . . ."

"Knowing that one of the horses has a tie-bar shoe is very helpful," Falcon said. "Thank you, Sue. That is a very good bit of information to know."

Sue beamed under the praise.

"And thank you, Jesse, Mr. and Mrs. Landers, for the meal and the information. You've all been a big help."

"Do you think you'll find them?" Mrs. Landers asked.

"Oh, I'll find them, all right," Falcon replied.

"But the country is so big," Mrs. Landers said.

"It's big, but there aren't that many places they can go. Besides, they'll be looking for me as hard as I'll be looking for them."

"Why will they be looking for you?"

Landers asked.

"Because they think I'm going to pay them a ransom for Andrew and Rosanna."

"Would you?" Mrs. Landers asked. "I mean, if that was the only way you could get your brother and sister back, would you pay a ransom for them?"

"Mrs. Landers, if I know for sure that paying a ransom would get them back, I would do so in a heartbeat. Their lives are worth much more than money to me. The problem is, even if I paid the ransom, I don't think they would let them go. So it has become a cat-and-mouse game. They are looking for me and the money. I'm looking for them and my brother and sister. We will find each other."

Falcon got up from the table. "I'd best be going. Again, I thank you for everything."

"Mr. MacCallister?"

"Yes, ma'am?"

"Thank you. It'll give us some peace knowin' that the killers of our boy are goin' to have to pay."

Falcon nodded, then went out the door.

CHAPTER TWENTY-THREE

With their horses tethered behind them, Andrew and Rosanna were lying on their stomachs. Andrew held the pistol stretched out in front of him with the hammer cocked.

"Don't frighten him off," Rosanna said.

"Shhh," Andrew replied.

Andrew pulled the trigger. The rabbit jumped once, then fell and lay very still.

"You got him!" Rosanna said excitedly.

"Yeah," Andrew said. "Now the only problem is going to be how to skin him without a knife."

"All you have to do is get it started. Then you can pull the skin off. Don't you remember Pa teaching us to do that?" Rosanna said.

"I remember how squeamish you were about it," Andrew teased.

Rosanna laughed. "You weren't exactly Daniel Boone," she said.

"I know, I didn't take to it all that well

either. But I'm glad Pa insisted that we do it, because now that I have to, I know that I can," Andrew answered. "That is, if I can get it started."

"How about the belt buckle?" Rosanna suggested.

"What?"

Rosanna pointed to the belt buckle on the pistol belt Andrew had taken from the albino. "I'll bet you could sharpen the edge of the buckle on a rock, then use it to get the skinning started."

Andrew smiled. "Good idea," he said.

"I don't know whether or not we can get a fire started by rubbing sticks together, though," Rosanna said. "That's what's worrying me."

"Don't you be worrying about that. I'll take care of it," Andrew said. He took off the pistol belt and handed it to Rosanna. "You start filing down the belt buckle."

Rosanna smiled at him. "You're enjoying this, aren't you?"

"Yes, in a rather perverse way, I am," Andrew said.

"Do you think you can actually get a fire started?"

"Let's just say that I believe your humble thespian will be sufficient to the task," Andrew replied.

As Rosanna found a rock and began filing the belt buckle, Andrew gathered wood for a fire. He also found two forked sticks, and a long, green limb to use as a skewer. Finally, he gathered a lot of dry grass and piled it up under a little tent of twigs.

"How are you coming on that belt buckle?"

"Pretty good. You can just about shave with it," Rosanna said, handing the buckle over to Andrew.

Andrew ran his thumb across it, then nodded in approval. Picking up the rabbit, he discovered, to his delight, that the buckle would work quite well. Using the sharpened edge, he sliced the skin down the belly, then pulled the skin off. After that, he cut open the belly and pulled out the intestines.

"Now," Rosanna said. "Let's see you rub those sticks together."

"I have a better idea," Andrew said.

Andrew pulled a shell from one of the loops on the pistol belt; then he separated the bullet from the shell casing. Punching one of the shells out of the pistol, he pushed the defanged cartridge into the empty chamber. Then, putting the barrel of the pistol in the dry grass, he pulled the trigger.

The muzzle flash ignited the dry grass, and by feeding it more grass and a few twigs, a fire was started.

"Oh, Andrew, that was brilliant!" Rosanna said, clapping her hands in delight.

"Yeah," Andrew said as he pushed the green willow skewer through the skinned and gutted rabbit. "It was, wasn't it?"

Andrew suspended the skewered rabbit over the open fire and within moments, the rabbit began browning and perfuming the air with the aroma of cooked meat.

"Now, if we could only come up with some way to duplicate Delmonico's *grande sauce de la viande,* the evening would be complete," Rosanna said.

"Forget Delmonico's meat sauce," Andrew replied. "I'd be satisfied with a little salt."

"Ah, who needs salt? Wasn't it Benjamin Franklin who said, 'Hunger is the best seasoning'?" Rosanna asked.

"I don't know who said it," Andrew said. "But we are about to put it to the test."

Andrew removed the rabbit from the skewer, then pulled it apart into two approximately even pieces. He handed one piece to Rosanna.

"Ohh," Rosanna said. "It is delicious."

"You see anything?" Loomis called up to Strayhorn.

Strayhorn was standing on the top of a

rocky precipice, looking back toward Eagle Pass.

"Nothing," Strayhorn called back down.

"That's funny. If they met at four o'clock like they was supposed to, they've had plenty of time to get here by now."

Loomis, Logan, and Strayhorn were at North Fork, where Beaver and Gopher Creeks joined. It was there that they were to meet Kelly and, presumably, Falcon MacCallister and the money. But though they had been here for a couple of hours, nobody had come.

"Loomis, you don't think Kelly would . . ." Strayhorn began, but he didn't finish.

"I don't think what?" Loomis replied. "You aren't going to ask me if I think Kelly would take the money and run out on us, are you, Logan? Because Kelly is my own brother, and I wouldn't like you thinking that."

"No — no, I wasn't goin' to say nothin' like that," Strayhorn said.

"Then what was you goin' to say?"

"I was just goin' to ask if you think maybe Kelly would have got into some kind of trouble, is all," Strayhorn said.

Loomis ran his hand through his hair and looked nervously toward the town.

"I don't know," he said. "Maybe. Logan,

do you see anything yet?"

"No," Logan called back down. "I don't see nothin'."

Loomis waited another few minutes, saying nothing as he paced back and forth nervously. Finally, he called up to Logan.

"Logan, come on down. Get mounted. We're goin'."

Logan picked his way down the side of the rock, then walked over to where the horses had been tethered. Loomis and Strayhorn were already mounted.

"Where are we goin'?" Logan asked.

"We're goin' into town. I'm going to find out what happened."

"Is that a good idea? I mean us goin' into town and all."

"Nobody but MacCallister would recognize us," Loomis said. "And if he is there, I want the son of a bitch to recognize us. We need to find him."

"And Kelly?" Logan asked.

"Yeah, and Kelly," Loomis replied almost as an afterthought.

It was late afternoon, just after the close of business, when they arrived, but the two saloons, the Long Trail and the Jayhawker, were already filling up with their evening trade.

Both saloons had a piano, and both pianos were banging away, resulting in a cacophony of discordant music, tumbling together in the middle of the street. From one of the saloons came a high-pitched scream. As it was followed immediately by an outbreak of laughter, it was obvious that the scream was not an expression of fear.

Loomis, Strayhorn, and Logan rode right down the middle of the street, the sounds of the hoofbeats echoing back from the buildings.

"My God, Loomis! Look over there!" Logan said.

"Look over where?"

"Over there, out front of the hardware store. You see that sign?"

Looking in the direction indicated by Logan, Loomis saw two wooden coffins, standing upright. They could see that there were bodies in both coffins, though, from this distance, they were too far away to see who the unfortunate occupants were.

But Loomis could read the large sign.

KILLED IN JUSTIFIABLE
HOMICIDE BY FALCON
MacCALISTER. IF NO-ONE
COMES TO CLAIM THESE TWO
BODIES, THEY WILL BE BURIED

IN POTTERS FIELD TOMORROW
AT TWO IN THE AFTERNOON.

Loomis angled his horse over toward the coffins. When he got closer, he could see who was in them. He did not recognize the first person.

"Loomis, look!" Logan said, pointing to the second coffin.

"Yeah." Loomis's voice was tight with anger. "I see him."

The person in the second coffin was his brother Kelly.

"I guess that means Kelly didn't get our money," Logan said.

"Money?" Loomis replied. "Goddamnit, Logan, that's Kelly in that coffin, and you're worryin' about money?"

"That is what we come to town for, ain't it? The money?" Logan said.

"And to find and kill MacCallister," Loomis said.

"Well hell, Loomis, there ain't really nothin' changed just 'cause MacCallister killed Kelly," Strayhorn said. "We was goin' to kill him and take the money before Kelly got hisself kilt. We're still goin' to kill him and take the money, ain't we?"

Loomis looked at his brother for a moment. Then he sighed and ran his hand through his hair. "Yeah," he finally said. "That's what we're goin' to do. Let's spread out and look through the town. If either of you see him, don't do nothin' yet. Come get the other two. I don't care how good the son of a bitch is. He can't beat all three of us together."

CHAPTER TWENTY-FOUR

When the albino opened his eyes, he wondered what he was doing sleeping on the floor. Then he realized he wasn't sleeping, he was on the floor because he had been knocked out. Somehow that Eastern dandy had managed to get himself untied.

He didn't have to wonder what he had been hit with. There were pieces of broken chair lying all around him.

The albino got up too fast, and a sudden wave of dizziness swept over him. He staggered over to the wall, then put his hand out to support himself until the dizziness passed. He was also nauseous and his head hurt. Putting his hand to the tender spot on his head, he came back with bloody fingers. The blood appeared especially bright red against the pallor of his skin.

Dropping his hand to his side, the albino realized that his gun was gone, and not only his gun, his gunbelt as well.

If Loomis and the others came back to find the prisoners gone, they wouldn't let him hear the end of it. It was bad enough that he had let some Eastern dandy and a woman make a fool of him; he wasn't going to wait around and let the others have their laughs at his expense. He was going after them, and he was going to bring them back.

The albino went out to the barn and saw that his horse was still there. So was his saddle. He allowed himself a smile.

"That was your first mistake. You should've taken my horse," he said aloud.

Going to his saddle, he opened one of the saddlebags and pulled out the gun and holster he had taken from the deputy when they escaped from jail back in Colorado Springs.

"And that was your second mistake. You should've checked my saddlebags," he added.

He pulled the pistol from the holster, then spun the cylinder, checking the loads.

"Now you are going to pay for being so dumb," he said as he took the saddle over to the horse and dropped it on the animal's back.

A few moments later, saddled and mounted, the albino rode out of the corral. For a moment, he was puzzled as to which was the best way to go; then he saw the tracks on the ground. Three sets of tracks trailed south, two sets went north.

Smiling, he slapped his legs against the side of his horse and broke into a gallop, heading north. A man and woman from New York, alone in the wilderness of Kansas — how far could they get anyway?

Logan and Strayhorn went into the Jayhawker Saloon, while Loomis went into the Long Trail. Loomis bought a beer, then moved around the bar listening in on the various conversations.

"Larry said he was leavin' the Doublecreek, said he was tired of cowboyin'."

"What's he goin' to do?"

"Said he was goin' to work at the livery for McGee."

Finding that conversation nonproductive, Loomis moved to another position. Here, they were arguing about how long it had been since the last rain.

One more move brought him success, when he heard MacCallister's name mentioned in the very first sentence.

"Where did MacCallister shoot that fella?"

"Which one are you talkin' about? Dunaway or Tate?"

"I know he shot the one in the middle of

the night in the hotel when he broke into his room. I'm talkin' about the second one, what was his name? Tate?"

"Yes, Kelly Tate, and MacCallister shot 'im over at Tinkers' Café. Him 'n Marshal Kingsley and Blanton was all havin' lunch together. Then Tate come in and Kingsley recognized him. So Kingsley goes over to say somethin' to him. Well, without so much as a fare-thee-well, Tate pulls his gun and kills poor ole Crack Kingsley. Then he turns his pistol toward the table where MacCallister and Blanton was sittin', and he commenced shootin' at them."

"And that's when MacCallister shot back," one of the other patrons said, denying the first patron the opportunity to finish.

"Damnit, Charley, I was tellin' this story," the first patron said.

"Well, hell, Frank, you was takin' forever to tell it," Charley said, and the others laughed.

"Well, I'll bet I can tell you why he commenced shootin' at MacCallister," Frank said.

"Prob'ly for the same reason Dunaway tried to take MacCallister on," Charley said. "I reckon he was just wantin' to make a name for himself for bein' the one that killed MacCallister. Only, he got hisself kilt instead."

"Nope," Frank said. "It was for the money."

"The money? What money? MacCallister ain't no wanted man. There ain't no dodgers out on him."

"No, not reward money. The ransom money."

"What ransom money? I ain't followin' you."

"Well, you know that MacCallister's brother and sister was took from the train last week, don't you?"

"Yeah, sure I know that. It was in the paper and all. Besides which, ever'one is talkin' about it."

"Uh-huh. Well, it turns out that this Tate fella that MacCallister kilt is one of the ones that took the MacCallisters."

"How do you know he was one of 'em?"

"I heard it from someone who was in the café when it all happened. It seems they had sent a letter to MacCallister askin' for a lot of ransom money to turn 'em a'loose. And MacCallister brung the money with him. Didn't you notice how he never let them saddlebags out of his sight?"

"Yeah, when he was in here I seen that he had 'em hangin' across his shoulder,"

Charley said. "Thought it was kind'a odd, but didn't give it that much thought."

"Well, sir, them saddlebags was stuffed with money, they was. Twenty thousand dollars in U.S. greenbacks. And Tate was supposed to pick up that money in exchange for MacCallister's brother and sister, only somethin' went wrong and he commenced a'shootin'. Next thing you know, Tate's dead, the brother and sister is still captured somewhere, and MacCallister is still carryin' around twenty thousand dollars."

"Twenty thousand dollars? All in them saddlebags? Lord, Lord, but ain't that a lot of money, though?"

"Wonder where at MacCallister got so much money," a third patron asked.

"Hell, Marty, don't you know?" Frank replied. "Falcon MacCallister is a rich man. A very rich man. For him to be carryin' twenty thousand dollars around in his saddlebags, would be like one of us carryin' two hundred dollars around."

"Hah!" Charley said. "If I scraped up all the money I had in the world, it wouldn't come to two hundred dollars."

"I hope you fellas don't mind my listenin' in to your palaver," Loomis said, speaking up for the first time. "But I'm a stranger here, and I don't mind tellin' you, that's

303

one ripsnorter of a story. You had a shootout in the street right here in town, did
you?"

"Wasn't on the street, it was over at Tinkers' Café," Charley said.

"And the shootout was over twenty thousand dollars?"

"Well, that's what Frank here is sayin',"
Charley said. "I figured it was because Tate
kilt our marshal."

" 'Cause the marshal figured out that Tate
was one of the ones that took them two actors who was MacCallister's brother and
sister," Marty said.

"For the ransom, which gets us back to
the twenty thousand dollars that MacCallister is carryin' around with him."

Loomis let out a whistle. "Twenty thousand dollars you say. That is a lot of money."

"Prob'ly 'bout as much as they got down
the street in the bank right now," Frank said.

Charley laughed. "And it wouldn't surprise me none if the money wasn't safer
hangin' in a saddlebag over MacCallister's
shoulder than it would be if it was in a
bank."

"Yeah," Marty agreed. "I'd hate to be the
one that tried to take the money from
Falcon MacCallister."

"Where at is this MacCallister fella now?"

Loomis asked.

"Why do you want to know?" Frank asked. He chuckled. "You ain't goin' to try and take it from him, are you?"

"I ain't that crazy," Loomis answered. He held up his finger to the bartender, signaling a refill for the three men. "It's just that I've never seen a man so rich he could carry twenty thousand dollars around in his saddlebags, and I'd like to see that."

Three new beers were put in front of Frank, Charley, and Marty.

"Thanks, Mr. . . ."

"Jones," Loomis said.

"Mr. Jones," Frank said, holding up his beer in salute.

"Well, Mr. Jones, if you're wantin' to see MacCallister, you ain't goin' to see him anywhere in Eagle Tail," Charley said. "If you want to see him, you need to find the lowlifes who took his sister and brother."

"Oh?"

"Yes, sir. Right after all the dust settled from the shootin' and all, MacCallister went out on the trail after them."

"Too bad," Loomis said. "I'd really like to see me a man that rich."

Loomis finished his drink, then with an amicable smile, left the Long Trail, and walked across the street to the Jayhawker.

CHAPTER TWENTY-FIVE

The Jayhawker did business with a rougher crowd than the Long Trail. The Long Trail was proud of its polished, mahogany bar and its gilt-edged mirror. The Jayhawker's bar was made of unpainted, ripsawed wood, and there were no towels or towel rings for the customers. There was a mirror behind the bar, but it wasn't gilt-edged, and all the images it showed were distorted by imperfections in the glass. There were perhaps half as many spittoons here as at the Long Trail, and whereas the ones at the Long Trail were polished brass, the spittoons here were pewter and looked as if they were rarely emptied, let alone cleaned. Unlike the clean floor at the Long Trail, the Jayhawker floor was riddled with expectorated tobacco quids and chewed cigar butts.

Even the bar girls showed the difference in quality as they were generally of riper years and more dispirited than the girls at the Long Trail.

Loomis looked around the room for a moment, squinting through the cloud of smoke. He saw Logan and Strayhorn sitting at a table in the back of the room. They were engaged in animated conversation with two other men. Loomis started toward them.

"Honey, you want to buy a girl a drink?" one of the bar girls asked, intercepting Loomis as he was crossing the floor.

Loomis looked at her. The dissipation from her trade had treated her badly. Her nose had been broken and she was missing a couple of teeth.

"Get away from me, you ugly old crone," Loomis snarled.

The woman's face reflected hurt, then anger, as she turned and walked away.

"I thought you two was supposed to be lookin' for someone," Loomis said to Logan and Strayhorn, ignoring the other two.

"Uh, he ain't in here," Logan said.

"I know he ain't. He ain't even in town," Loomis said. "Who are these men?" He glared at the two men who were sharing the table with Strayhorn and Logan.

"This here is Luke, and this is Seth," Strayhorn said by way of introduction. "They're good men."

"How do you know they are good men?"

"Well, I've rode with Seth before," Stray-horn said. "I don't know Luke, he's a local, but Seth has spoke good of him, and if he's good enough for Seth, then he's all right by me."

"Yeah, well, I don't know either one of them," Loomis said.

"I know'd your brother Kelly," Seth said. "Me 'n him was pards once, and it pained me to see him standin' in the coffin' out there for the whole town to gawk at."

Seth had a beard. Luke didn't actually have a beard, but was sporting what looked to be about a five-day growth.

"So, you know Kelly, huh?"

"Yep. It's been a while back, but I know'd him all right."

"He never mentioned you to me," Loomis replied.

"I don't doubt that he didn't say nothin' about me. Last time he seen me, I was lyin' gut-shot on the streets of Boulder. I guess he figured I died. Don't many folks survive bein' gut-shot."

"How well did you know him?"

Seth grinned, then pointed to Loomis's drooping eye. "I know'd him well enough to know how you come by that droopin' eye," he said.

"Oh? How?"

"Your other brother, Drew, hit you in the face with a shovel when you was all kids," Seth said.

That was true, and what's more, Seth would have had to learn it from Kelly, because Loomis had never shared the story with anyone.

"Damn!" Strayhorn said, laughing. "Is that true? Did Drew really hit you with a shovel?"

"Yeah," Loomis said. "It's true."

"Strayhorn tells me that MacCallister is also the one that kilt Drew," Seth said.

"That's right."

"Seems to me like this MacCallister fella is whittlin' your family down pretty good," Seth said. "First Drew, then Kelly. I wouldn't doubt but what he has his sights set on you now."

"Yeah, well, that's just fine," Loomis said. "Because I have my sights on him."

"Yeah, well, I wouldn't mind gettin' him in my sights my ownself. Course, he never kilt no brother of mine or nothin' like that, but he did kill a pard, and I'd like to pay him back."

"Do you think he's got the money?" Luke asked.

"What money?" Loomis asked.

"The ransom money you was askin' for to

get his brother and sister back," Luke replied.

"What the hell?" Loomis said in obvious irritation. He looked at both Strayhorn and Logan. "Is there any part of our business you two haven't been blabberin' about? Think maybe we ought to go down to the newspaper office so they can print the story?"

"It wasn't just blabberin', Loomis," Strayhorn said.

"It wasn't? I'd like to know what it was then," Loomis said.

"It was recruitin'."

"Recruitin'? What do you mean it was recruitin'?"

"Well, it's like this," Strayhorn explained. "Me 'n Logan here was talkin' it over and . . ."

"You and Logan was talkin' it over, was you?" Loomis said, his voice dripping with sarcasm.

"Yeah," Strayhorn said, not catching the sarcasm in Loomis's voice. "We was talkin' it over and we decided it might not be a bad idea to let Seth and Luke in on our job."

"And why would we want to do that?" Loomis asked.

" 'Cause of MacCallister," Strayhorn said. "I mean, he's done kilt both your brothers.

310

I don't know how the fight went between MacCallister and Kelly, but I seen him with Drew. Hell, you seen him with Drew, too. And Drew was 'bout the fastest with a gun I ever seen, until I seen MacCallister."

"Strayhorn's right, Loomis," Logan said. "I wouldn't want to go up agin' MacCallister with just the three of us and the albino. I mean, there was five of us last time and he got the better of us."

Loomis stroked his chin and studied Seth and Luke for a moment.

"I reckon you'd want a cut of the money if you come in," he said.

"Well, yeah," Seth answered. "I mean, if we're goin' to be a part of it, we'd like our cut."

"Is this what you both want?" Loomis asked Strayhorn and Logan.

"Yeah," the two men said.

"All right."

"Good!"

Strayhorn and Logan shook hands with Seth and Luke.

"Only, I should tell you that their money is goin' to be comin' from your cut," Loomis said to Strayhorn and Logan. "I ain't givin' up none of my money."

"Wait a minute," Logan said. "That ain't no way fair."

"Fair or not, that's the way it's goin' to be," Loomis said. "So, you can take it or leave it."

"How much money are we talkin' about here?" Luke asked.

"Twenty thousand dollars," Logan said.

"Twenty thousand?" Luke said. "My God, that's all the money there is in the world."

"I get half of it," Loomis said. "You boys can split up what's left."

"Why do you get half?" Seth asked.

"Because it was my idea," Loomis said. "Now, that's the terms. Are you in or not?"

"That'd still be two thousand dollars apiece, Seth," Luke said. "I ain't never had no two thousand dollars in my whole life. Have you?"

Seth shook his head. "No," he said. "No, I ain't."

"I say let's do it."

Seth thought for a moment before he replied. "Is this money for real? I mean, does Falcon MacCallister actually have that kind of money?"

"Yeah, he has that kind of money. Fact is, he has that money on him right now."

"What?" Strayhorn asked. "How do you know he has that kind of money on him now?"

"He's carrying it around with him in a

pair of saddlebags," Loomis said. "I heard 'em talkin' about it over at the Long Trail."

"Twenty thousand dollars in saddlebags," Logan said. "Think of that."

"So, what do we do next?" Seth asked.

"Next, we go back to the way station, take care of some business there, then pick up the albino and start trailing MacCallister."

"What about . . ." Strayhorn said. Then, he paused in mid-sentence and looked around the saloon to make certain no one was close enough to overhear what he was saying.

"What about what?" Loomis asked.

"You know," Strayhorn said. "The — uh — people we have there. What are we going to do with them?"

"We're going to take care of them," Loomis said. "We don't need them as insurance anymore. We know that MacCallister has the money. All we have to do is find him."

"It seems a shame to — uh — well, I mean, the woman is so pretty, it seems like a waste to just — take care of her."

Loomis smiled. "I didn't say we wouldn't have a little fun first," he said.

"Oh, Loomis, I don't know," Logan said.

"What do you mean, you don't know?"

"There's six of us."

"There was five of us back at the farm,

and that went all right."

"Yes, but there was two women there. Well, a girl and a woman. Here, there is just one woman."

Loomis looked over at the soiled dove who had approached him when he first came into the saloon.

"Hey, you," he called. "Come here."

The woman, who was probably no older than thirty, but who looked fifty, flashed a gap-toothed smile at being summoned. She hurried over to the table.

"There's five of us here," Loomis said. "If we paid you to go upstairs with us, could you handle all five of us?"

"Good Lord, you don't mean at the same time, do you?" the soiled dove answered, her eyes wide with wonder.

"No, no, not at the same time," Loomis said. "My question is, could you handle all five of us one at a time?"

"Yes."

"What if we had one more friend?"

"All of you will pay?"

"Yes."

The girl nodded. "Yes, I could handle all six of you."

"What's the most number of men you've ever done in one night?"

"Nineteen."

"All right, thanks," Loomis said.

"So, are we going up?"

"Do you really think I would want to share the sheets with someone as ugly as you are?" Loomis asked. He made a dismissive motion with his hand. "Go away."

Suddenly, and unexpectedly, the woman's eyes filled with tears.

"I'll be damned," Seth said. "Look at that. I don't think I ever seen a whore cry before."

"Go away," Loomis said again.

"You are an incredibly cruel man," the woman said as she turned and walked away.

"Still worried about whether one woman can handle all of us?" Loomis asked Logan.

"No, I guess not," Logan said.

Loomis stood up. "Come on, let's go. It'll be dark by the time we get there as it is. Too much later and the albino is likely to take a few shots at us."

Leaving the saloon, the five men mounted their horses, then rode out of town. As they left, they passed the two coffins, along with the sign saying that, if not claimed, Loomis's brother Kelly and Dunaway would be buried in Potter's Field the next day.

Loomis didn't even bother to look in the direction of his brother.

CHAPTER TWENTY-SIX

"There's a house," Rosanna said, pointing to a structure in the gathering shadows.

"Thank God," Andrew said, smiling broadly. "I hope they have some coffee!" He urged his horse into a trot.

"Andrew, wait," Rosanna called to him.

"Wait? Wait for what?"

"I don't think there is anyone there."

"Well, we aren't going to stand around on niceties, Rosanna. We're going in, whether there is anyone home or not."

As they got closer to the house, more and more details began to be revealed, such as a barn with no door, a corral with no horses, and a fence with no gate. There was the remnant of a garden, and a couple of windows were broken out.

"It doesn't look like we are going to have to worry about being invited in," Andrew said. "I don't think anyone lives here."

"I don't think so either," Rosanna said.

They rode on into the front yard, or what had once been the front yard.

"Hello the house!" Andrew called.

There was no response to his call.

"Hello the house!" he called again.

"Andrew, let's keep going," Rosanna suggested.

"Why?"

"I don't know. Something about this house frightens me," she said.

Andrew laughed.

"What is so funny?"

"We were taken off a train in the middle of the night, we have killers after us, and you are scared of an empty house."

Rosanna laughed as well. "Yeah," she said. "You're right."

Andrew dismounted.

"What are you doing?"

"I'm going to go inside and have a look around," he said.

Rosanna dismounted as well. "All right, if you're going in, I am, too."

They tied their horses to what remained of the front fence, then walked up to the house.

"Careful of the first step, it's broken," Rosanna pointed out.

The two went inside. As they had expected, the house was totally deserted, with not one piece of furniture.

Andrew chuckled.

"What's so funny?"

"So much for my cup of coffee," he said.

An old newspaper was lying on the floor and Andrew picked it up.

"Look at this," he said. "It says raids along the Kansas-Missouri border are continuing."

"What raids?" Rosanna asked.

"It's talking about the Civil War. This paper is dated April 1862."

"Oh, my. This house has been empty a very long time," Rosanna said.

Suddenly, there was the sound of tinkling glass, then the buzz of a bullet whizzing by and plunking into the wall behind them. The sound of a rifle shot rolled into the room.

"What?" Rosanna said.

"Get down! Someone is shooting at us!" Andrew shouted.

Both dropped to the floor just as a second shot crashed through the window.

"Are you all right?" Andrew asked.

"Yes."

"You crawl over into the corner, away from the windows," Andrew said.

"What are you going to do?"

"I'm going to shoot back," Andrew said,

pulling his pistol.

The albino cursed himself for missing. Of course, with the failing light, it wasn't that easy of a shot. But he should have taken a little more time, aimed a bit more carefully.

He jacked another round into the rifle and fired a third time, even though he had no target in sight.

"You two come out of there!" the albino shouted.

He heard the crash of glass, then a pistol shot. The bullet from the pistol didn't come anywhere close and he laughed.

"I reckon not all you MacCallisters can shoot!" he called out to them.

He fired again into the house and, once more, his rifle shot was answered with an ineffective pistol shot.

"If you folks don't come out of there right now, I'm going to burn you out!" the albino called. "You can see how dry the wood is. That ole house will go up like a prairie fire."

"Can he burn us out?" Rosanna asked, her voice betraying her fright.

"Not if we stop him," Andrew replied.

"How are we going to stop him?"

"By killing him," Andrew said resolutely. "I should have done that when I had the

319

chance."

"Do you think you can shoot him from here?"

Andrew held up the pistol and looked at it. "No," he said. "Not with this. Not unless we do something drastic."

"Like what?"

"Did you hear what I said?" the albino's voice floated in to them. "If you don't come out of there now, I'm going to burn you out."

"I've got an idea," Andrew said.

The albino looked down at the house. It was still light, but the sun had already dipped below the western horizon. It would be dark soon. If he didn't do something fast, they could sneak away in the night. He started studying the best way to move up to the house and set fire to it.

Then, as he was contemplating the best route of approach, the front door of the house opened, and the man came running out.

"Andrew, no! Don't leave me!" he heard the woman scream.

"I'm getting out of here! You're on your own!" Andrew shouted back as he ran toward the horses that were tied out front. He held the pistol out and fired a couple of ineffective rounds toward the albino.

"Andrew, you coward!" Rosanna screamed.

"Well now," the albino said out loud, chuckling at the drama playing out before him. "I reckon a coward like you needs killin'."

The albino raised his rifle and fired. Andrew grabbed his chest, spun, then went down.

"Andrew, no! No!" Rosanna shouted. She came running out of the house and knelt on the ground beside him, crying uncontrollably. "You killed him! You killed him!"

The albino grabbed the rifle by the barrel and held it across his shoulder as he sauntered down, leisurely, to where the woman was crying over her brother.

"Why are you cryin' over him, missy? It looked to me like he was runnin' out on you," the albino said. He came up to within about five feet of the weeping woman and the prostrate man. "I'd say he got what was good for him."

"No, you don't understand," Rosanna said. "He was a fine, sensitive man. We should have never come to this — this savage place."

"Yeah, well, you did come," the albino said. "Now, what do you say me 'n you go back in the house and have us a little fun?"

"Fun? You think I could be with you after you what you just did to my brother? How can you kill a man in cold blood like that?" Rosanna asked, getting to her feet and stepping away from Andrew.

"Your brother was no man. He was a worm," the albino said.

Suddenly Andrew rolled over, a cocked pistol in his hand. He pointed it at the albino.

"The smallest worm will turn, being trodden upon," Andrew said.

"What?"

"That is a quote from Shakespeare, *King Henry the Fourth,* Act Five, Scene Six," Andrew explained.

"You son of a . . ." the albino shouted, dropping his rifle and making a grab for his pistol. That was as far as he got before Andrew pulled the trigger.

The bullet hit the albino in the gut and he slapped his hand over the wound. Blood began spilling through his fingers.

"You shot me," he said in disbelief. "I can't believe I was shot by someone like you."

"And just when you thought you had it all going your way," Andrew replied.

The albino fell on his back, gasped a

couple of times, then lay still.

"Is he dead?" Rosanna asked.

As Andrew looked at the albino's face, a strange thing happened. The eyes, which were pink, gradually deepened in color until they were a very bright blood red. Andrew felt of his pulse, and found none.

"He's dead."

"Good," Rosanna said. "I never thought I would feel joy over the death of another human being, but I must confess that . . ." Rosanna paused in mid-sentence, then looked out into the gathering darkness. "Andrew!"

"What?"

"Someone is coming!"

"Quick, back into the house!" Andrew said, and the two of them scurried back inside. It was quite dark inside the house now, and Andrew knew that he could stand in the window without being seen, while there was still enough light to keep an eye on the approaching rider.

Andrew watched as the rider came closer; then he called out.

"That's far enough, mister!"

"What's the matter, Andrew?" the rider called back. "Don't you recognize your own brother?"

"Falcon!" Andrew shouted excitedly.

"Rosanna, it's Falcon!"

Andrew and Rosanna ran outside just as Falcon rode up to the front of the house and dismounted. Rosanna rushed into his arms to embrace and kiss him. Andrew shook his hand.

After the greeting, Falcon looked down at the albino's body.

"You did this?" he asked.

"Andrew did," Rosanna answered proudly.

"We both did it," Andrew said. "Rosanna did a superb job of acting."

"Acting?" Falcon replied. Then, with a laugh, he shook his head. "Never mind, I'm not even going to ask."

"How did you find us?" Andrew asked.

"I tracked you to the way station. Saw a broken chair and some loose rope there, then saw that three horses came this way and three went the other, so I figured out what happened."

"How did you know which horse to follow?"

"Because of Pretty," Falcon replied.

"Pretty?"

Smiling, Falcon looked over at the two horses Andrew and Rosanna had ridden. One was a mare, and Falcon lifted the mare's left forefoot.

"This is Pretty. She has a tie-bar shoe," he

said. He went on to explain how he had visited the Landers family and learned the horse's name. "And of course, there was this," he said, holding up the little piece of cloth that Rosanna had torn from her dress and tied to the branch of the willow tree.

"I told you he would find it," Rosanna said to Andrew.

"You were right," Andrew admitted.

"Falcon, you wouldn't have any water with you, would you?" Rosanna asked. "We haven't had a drop to drink since we escaped."

Falcon took his canteen down and handed it over. Both Rosanna and Andrew drank deeply.

"I'm afraid we drank all of it," Andrew said, returning the empty canteen.

"That's all right, we'll get some more at the hotel."

"The hotel? What hotel?"

"The hotel in Gem. It's not too far from here. We'll spend the night there."

"You mean a real hotel? With beds and sheets and a bath?" Rosanna asked.

"Well, it's nothing like the Bixby Hotel," Falcon said, referring to the hotel he had stayed in during his last visit to New York. He nodded toward the old, deserted house.

"But I'm reasonably sure it will beat this place."

"What will we do with him?" Andrew asked, nodding toward the albino's body.

"If you are asking me, I would say leave the son of a bitch here," Falcon said.

"Falcon, we can't just leave him here," Rosanna said.

"Why not?"

"I just wouldn't feel right about it," Rosanna said.

"Believe me, it won't bother him any."

"I wouldn't feel right about it either," Andrew said.

Falcon chuckled, and shook his head. "Oh, my civilized siblings," he said. "All right, if it will make you feel any better, when we get to town, we'll pay the undertaker to come get him."

"Won't we have to see the sheriff and explain why we killed him?"

Falcon laughed.

"What is it?"

"There is no sheriff in Gem. There is no law of any kind except from the county seat in Colby."

"Won't we need to explain this to him?"

"Not much of an explanation needed. The story about you two getting taken off the train ran in every paper in the West. Hell, probably in just about every paper in the U.S. and Europe."

"You really think so?" Andrew asked.

"I'm sure of it."

"Wow," he said, his eyes sparking in excitement.

"What is it, Andrew? What are you thinking?" Rosanna asked.

"I'm thinking about the publicity," Andrew said. "Can you imagine what that will do for our box office?"

Rosanna laughed. "You are incorrigible."

CHAPTER TWENTY-SEVEN

The town of Gem was little more than a small cluster of buildings rising from the prairie in front of them. Night had fallen by the time they arrived, but it was not so late that the town itself was dark. Nearly every house had light, ranging from the dim, golden gleam of candles in the smaller houses, to the brighter glow of lanterns in the more substantial homes, as well as the café and saloon.

There was a post sticking up in the middle of the crossroads, right in the center of the town. The sign identified the two main streets of Gem as Lincoln and Pine.

"Where is this hotel you were talking about?" Rosanna asked.

"I imagine that's it," Falcon said, pointing to a ramshackle building that was somewhat larger than the others. A porch roof protruded from the front of the building, and on the roof was a sign that had clearly been broken in half, probably by a strong gust of wind. The sign read: TEL.

"You're right," Rosanna said with a sigh. "It isn't the Bixby."

"We could have stayed back at the deserted house," Falcon teased.

"No, no, I'm not complaining," Rosanna said.

"A bill of fare?" the waiter asked in response to Rosanna's request.

The first thing they had done after securing a room, was go to Aunt Emma's Café.

"A menu," Rosanna explained.

"Oh. We don't have a menu, ma'am."

"What do you have?"

"We have ham, eggs, and potatoes," the waiter said. "Oh, and biscuits."

Rosanna smiled sweetly. "It sounds delightful," she said. "I believe I will have ham, eggs, and potatoes. Oh, and biscuits," she added.

"Yes, ma'am," the waiter replied, unaware of the sarcasm of her response. "And you gentlemen?"

"That sounds good to me," Andrew said with a little chuckle.

Falcon just nodded, and the waiter left to fill their orders.

"What do we do tomorrow?" Rosanna

asked after the waiter left.

"First thing tomorrow, I'll take you two back to the railroad where you can catch the train and finish your trip to New York," Falcon said.

"Then you're going back to the Valley?" Andrew asked, referring to MacCallister Valley.

Falcon shook his head. "Not right away."

"What do you mean, not right away?" Rosanna asked. "What else do you have to do?"

"I just need to take care of a little business, that's all."

"I want to help," Andrew said, looking directly at Falcon.

"No."

"Help? Help what?" Rosanna asked. "What's going on here?"

"When Falcon says he is going to take care of a little business, he's talking about the men who pulled us from the train. Right, little brother?"

"Yes."

"Whatever beef you have with them, mine is larger," Andrew said.

"Oh," Rosanna said.

"I want to help."

"Andrew, these men are killers," Falcon said. "You aren't cut out for anything like this. I couldn't live with myself if anything happened to either of you."

"Falcon, I'm Jamie's son, same as you," Andrew said. "And I'm going to take part in this with you, or despite you."

There was an edge of resolve in his brother's voice that reminded Falcon of his father, and despite himself, he smiled. He reached out with his hand and put it on Andrew's shoulder.

"All right, brother," he said. "I'd be proud to have you by my side."

After supper, Falcon found the town undertaker, identified himself, then paid to have the undertaker go out to retrieve the albino's body. That taken care of, he returned to the hotel, knocked on the doors of both Andrew and Rosanna to make certain they were all right, then went to his own room.

Lying in bed, watching moon patterns on the wall of his room, Falcon had a feeling that, tomorrow, everything would be coming to a head. He would rather Andrew not be with him, but he could understand Andrew's need to participate. He just hoped that Andrew lived through it.

"Lord," he said, praying aloud. "If there is anything to the idea that those who've gone on can look down on us and take care of us, I want you to let Pa take particular care of Andrew."

It wasn't until the next morning that a wagon left Gem to bring the albino's body back. The sign painted on the side of the wagon read: EBENEZER POSEY — MORTUARY SERVICES.

It was an ordinary farm wagon, pulled by a team of mules, and it was what Ebenezer used when he called for a recently deceased in the home. It wasn't until afterward, after the embalming and dressing them in their funeral clothes, then putting them in coffins, that he would use the glass-sided, highly polished black hearse. The hearse was pulled by a pair of matching black horses, and Ebenezer would dress in a cutaway jacket, striped pants, ruffled shirt, tie, and high hat to drive it. He only used the hearse if there was to be an actual funeral. And from what he knew of these remains, there would be no funeral, just a burial in poorly marked grave.

But from the moment Falcon MacCallister approached him about retrieving the body, Ebenezer was more than willing to do it. He had read about the two famous actors being taken from the train. He also knew who Falcon MacCallister was, and by burying one of the men responsible for such a heinous crime, he felt as if he was reaching out to touch history. And, of course, it didn't hurt that Falcon had paid him generously to see to the body.

He knew exactly where the body was. It was at the old Dumey house, which was about eight miles west by southwest of Gem. It had been twenty years since anyone had lived in the Dumey house. In fact, one of Ebenezer's first jobs had been to remove Mrs. Ella Dumey from this very house when she died. She was the last occupant.

As Ebenezer drove his wagon out to the house, he tried to think of some way he could use this job to his advantage. It was interesting to be a part of history like this, but he wondered if there wasn't also some way he could profit from it. Maybe he could put the body on display and charge a nickel apiece to anyone who wanted to see it.

Of course, some would think that was wrong, but it wasn't like a regular viewing. He was sure that the deceased, whoever he was, would have no family or friends coming to see him. The only people who would be interested would be the morbidly curious, and Ebenezer saw nothing wrong with charging them a small fee.

He saw the old house as soon as he came

over the hill, and he saw buzzards circling about. He hoped they hadn't torn too much flesh away from the face. It would make it harder for him to prepare the body for viewing.

As he got a little closer, he picked up a shotgun and fired it toward the buzzards. He didn't hit any of them, but he wasn't aiming at them. All he wanted to do was scare them away, and that he did.

Ebenezer pulled into the yard, set the brake on the wagon, then climbed down to have a look at the body.

He gasped, not because of anything the buzzards had done, because they had done nothing. It might have been better if they had.

This man's face was as white as chalk, and his eyes, which were wide open, were as red as cherries. Ebenezer had seen the pallor of death hundreds of times during his career. But he had never seen anything like what he was looking at now. The sight was so bizarre that it made him shiver.

"Who's going to pay to look at something like this?" he asked aloud.

Then, almost as soon as he asked the question, he had second thoughts. This was not only one of the ones who took the Mac-Callisters from the train. This fella looked like some sort of monster.

"Yes," he said aloud. "As frightening as you look, I'll just bet folks will come from all around to see you! Why, you could turn into a gold mine!"

Ebenezer lowered the tailgate of the wagon, then started examining the body to figure out the best way to get him into the wagon. With rigor mortis setting in, it might be easier not to try and lift him, but just grab him by one of his arms and pull him into the wagon.

"Ha! There's someone down there! I told you they would be at the old Dumey House," Luke said as he, Loomis, Seth, Strayhorn, and Logan crested a little hill and the old farmhouse came into view.

"That ain't them," Loomis said.

"What do you mean it ain't them? There don't nobody live at the Dumey house anymore so that has to be them."

"Where'd they get the wagon?"

"Yeah, that's right," Strayhorn said. "They didn't have no wagon."

"Well, it's somebody," Luke said.

"Yeah, but who?" Logan asked.

"When we get down there, don't nobody do no talkin' but me," Loomis ordered.

■ ■ ■ ■

Ebenezer had just gotten the body into the back of the wagon, and the tarp pulled over it, when he saw the five riders coming toward him. They were nearly upon him, and he was startled that they had managed to get so close without him seeing them.

"Good mornin'," one of the riders said. The man who spoke had a drooping eye and a pockmarked face. "Who might you be?"

"Good mornin'. Ebenezer Posey is my name. Who are you fellas?"

"My name's Jones," Loomis said. He pointed to the sign on the wagon. "I see you are an undertaker."

"Yes, sir, I am."

"Do you have a body in the wagon?"

"Indeed I do, sir. And you may have heard of him."

"Really? Who is it? What's his name?"

"Oh," Ebenezer said. "Well, I don't actually know his name. What I mean when I say you may have heard of him is that he was one of the outlaws who took those famous actors off the train a few days ago. Perhaps you read about it?"

"Yes, yes, we did read about it."

"Well, sir, justice has been done. At least

in the case of this one man. Because the MacCallisters are free, and this man, one of their captors, is dead."

"Do you think we could take a look at him?" Loomis asked.

"Well, I — uh," Ebenezer began. He had planned to charge a nickel apiece for people to view the body, and this would be a chance to try it out. On the other hand, there were five of them, and he was alone, and a long way from town.

Deciding that discretion was the better part of valor, Ebenezer nodded.

"I suppose you can," he said as he pulled the cover down.

"Damn! It's the albino!" Logan said.

Ebenezer squinted in curiosity. "Do you know this man, sir?" he asked.

"No," Loomis said, speaking quickly before Logan could answer. "It's just that the man is an albino. I guess my friend has never seen one before."

"Yes," Ebenezer said, looking at the chalk-white face. "Yes, death does drain one of color, but I must say that, in this case, the result has been quite dramatic. Perhaps he was an albino."

"How do you know this is one of the men who took the MacCallisters?" Loomis asked.

"Oh, the MacCallisters themselves told me," Ebenezer said. "They, and their brother, came into town last night. Mr. Falcon MacCallister himself made the arrangements. I — uh — didn't come out until this morning, because I was certain the deceased wouldn't be going anywhere during the night."

Ebenezer chuckled at his own joke, but stopped when he realized that nobody was laughing with him.

"You said town," Loomis said. "What town would that be?"

"Oh, it's Gem," Ebenezer said. He pointed. "It's about seven or eight miles in that direction. You can't miss it, it's the only town for miles around. Most folks figured the railroad would come through the town so it built up real quick. Course, the railroad didn't come through, so now we purt' near got more buildin's than we got people." He chuckled. "I reckon havin' all them Mac-Callisters come to town at the same time is about the most excitin' thing that ever happened to Gem."

"Are they still there?" Loomis asked.

"Yes, sir, they sure are. I think they plan to hang around for a few days until Miss MacCallister is somewhat recovered from her ordeal."

"I see. Tell me, is there a saloon in town?"

"Indeed there is," Ebenezer said. "It's called The Farmers' Dell, and it's quite good."

"Boys, it's been a long hot ride," Loomis said. "What do you say we ride into town and have ourselves a few beers?"

"Have a few beers? Is that all we're goin' to do is just have a few beers? What about . . . ?" Logan asked, but a sharp glance from Loomis cut him off.

Loomis touched the brim of his hat by way of goodbye to Posey, then led the others in the direction of town.

"I wonder what happened to the albino," Logan said after they were out of earshot.

"He got hisself kilt," Strayhorn replied.

"Yeah, we could all see that. But the question is, who done it?"

"What do you mean, who done it? Falcon MacCallister done it," Loomis said.

"Could be that one of them actors done it," Logan said. "If I'd had a chance to talk to that undertaker any longer, I would'a asked him who done it."

"You talked too much already," Loomis said. "It's a wonder you didn't give us up when you said that was the albino."

"Sorry, Loomis. I guess I just wasn't thinkin'," Logan said.

339

"What are we goin' to do when we get to town?" Seth asked.

"We're goin' to kill the MacCallisters, take the money, and leave," Loomis answered.

"Just like that?"

"Just like that. You heard what that old coot said about Gem. He said the town is about dried up. Is that right, Luke? You're from here. What's Gem like?"

"Like Posey said, there ain't much to the town," Luke said.

"Sounds like our kind of town," Loomis said. He smiled. "As a matter of fact, after we get rid of the MacCallisters, we may just take it over. I always wanted me a town."

CHAPTER TWENTY-EIGHT

When Loomis and the others reached the edge of town, they stopped. There was not one soul to be seen.

"What is this?" Strayhorn asked. "Is this a ghost town?"

"No," Loomis said. "Look at the buildings. They all have glass, some of 'em is fresh-painted. This is no ghost town."

"Then where at is ever'body?"

"I don't know," Loomis said.

"I don't like it. It's givin' me the willies," Logan said.

"Ever'thing gives you the willies," Loomis replied, gruffly.

"Loomis, look!" Strayhorn said.

Logan pointed to the front of a hardware store. There were six coffins standing up in front of the store. Three of them were closed, and on the front of the closed coffins were three signs:

DREW TATE
KELLY TATE
THE ALBINO

There were signs on the empty coffins as well. These signs read:

LOOMIS TATE
MATT LOGAN
KEN STRAYHORN

"What's going on here?" Loomis shouted, pulling his pistol.

"They don't have no coffins for Seth and Luke. They must not know about them," Strayhorn said.

"Shut up," Loomis said.

"There's the saloon," Luke said. "I need a drink."

"Get the horses off the street first," Loomis said.

"Where?"

Loomis pointed toward a gap between the apothecary and a feed store. "Take 'em back there," he said.

"Why are we puttin' our horses back here?" Logan asked as they tied their horses off behind the apothecary.

"Think about it," Loomis said. "There ain't another horse in sight. We leave ours

342

tied up out there, they'll stick out like a sore thumb. I don't know what's goin' on here, but I think we should play it careful."

"What about the saloon?" Strayhorn asked. "Can we go into the saloon?"

"Yeah," Loomis said. "If it's open, then someone is bound to be in there, even if it is just the bartender."

The five men walked back out to the front of the apothecary, then across the street to the saloon. Strayhorn pushed open the batwing doors, then looked around.

The saloon was empty.

"They's nobody in here!" he called back to the others.

"What do you mean they's nobody in here?" Loomis said, coming in behind him. "There's got to be somebody in here. Where's the bartender?"

Logan, Seth, and Luke came in as well, and they stood there for a moment, looking around the empty saloon.

"Look," Logan said, pointing to a table. There were four hands of cards lying on the table, and a stack of chips in the middle of the table, as well as stacks in front of each hand.

"They left their money," Strayhorn said. He took his hat off and went over to start raking the chips off the table.

"What are you doing?" Loomis asked.

"I'm takin' this money," Strayhorn said.

"Where do you plan to spend it, fool?" Loomis asked. "That ain't real money, that's just poker chips. They ain't worth a nickel outside this saloon."

"Oh," Strayhorn said, crestfallen. "Oh, yeah, I reckon you're right." He dumped the chips back onto the table.

"Hey, Loomis, what do you make of that?" Seth asked, pointing to the bar.

There, sitting on the bar, were two bottles of whiskey.

There was a sign leaning against the whiskey bottles.

Drink up Boys, they are on Me.
     ~ FALCON MACCALLISTER.

"Well, that's nice of him," Strayhorn said. He pulled the cork, then turned the bottle up to his lips, taking several deep swallows. Then, he set the bottle back on the bar and wiped his mouth with the back of his hand.

"That wasn't very smart," Loomis said. "He probably poisoned it."

"What?" Strayhorn gasped. He staggered back against the bar and stood there for a second with his hands clasped over his stomach.

344

"What about it, Strayhorn?" Logan asked. "Is it poison?"

Strayhorn took several deep breaths. Then he smiled. "Nah," he said. "It ain't poison."

Strayhorn reached for the bottle again, but Logan beat him to it.

"You had your drink," Logan said.

Suddenly the clock whirred, then began to chime, but Loomis turned and shot it, stopping the clock in mid-chime.

Luke laughed.

"What's so damn funny?" Loomis asked.

"You just killed the clock," Luke said.

"Yeah, and I'll kill you if you don't shut up."

"I was just funnin' with you, Loomis," Luke said. "I didn't mean nothin' by it."

By now the second bottle had been opened, and the men were passing it back and forth as well.

"I don't like this," Loomis said. "I don't like this at all."

"Hell, have a drink, Loomis," Strayhorn said. "It's easy enough to figure out what's happened."

"What has happened?"

"MacCallister heard we was comin' and him and his brother and sister skedaddled out of town, that's all. They're afraid of us."

"Uh-huh? Where is the rest of the town?"

Loomis asked.

Falcon, Andrew, and Rosanna were in Falcon's hotel room. They had chosen it because it was at the front of the hotel, and had a commanding view of both Lincoln and Pine Streets. It also had a view of The Farmers' Dell Saloon.

"Everyone is in the church?" Falcon asked.

"Yes," Andrew answered. "Everyone except Posey, the undertaker. And we've got somebody out on the road to meet him, to keep him from comin' into town till it's all over."

"Good," Falcon said. "This is our fight, not the town's fight. This way, no one will get hurt."

"Where are they now, Rosanna?" Andrew asked.

"They're still in the saloon," Rosanna said. She was looking through the window.

"Are you ready?" Falcon asked.

"I'm ready," Rosanna answered.

"How about you?" Falcon asked Andrew.

"I'm ready."

"Then let's do it."

Nodding, Rosanna raised the window and stepped out onto the porch roof. She walked to the edge of the porch, then shielded her eyes with her hands, looking toward the end of Lincoln Street.

"Loomis, come here, look at this!" Strayhorn called. Strayhorn was standing at the door of the saloon.

"What?"

"It's the MacCallister woman," Strayhorn said.

Loomis hurried quickly to the door.

"I don't see anyone coming!"

They heard the woman's voice floating across the street.

"All right, I'll look that way," she said.

"Son of a bitch! They are in the hotel waitin' for us," Loomis said. "They didn't see us come in!"

"Well, if they're countin' on her to give 'em warnin', they got another think comin'," Strayhorn said. He aimed at the woman.

"No!" Loomis said, knocking his hand down. "You'll give us away."

"You got a plan?"

"Yeah."

"What is it?"

"Follow me."

With guns drawn, the five men left through the back door of the saloon, ran up the alley to the far end of the street, then dashed across the street and came back down another alley until they were behind the hotel.

The back door of the hotel was unlocked.

"You know which room they're in?" Seth whispered.

"It has to be the upstairs front room," Loomis answered just as quietly. "She was talkin' to someone in there."

The five men went up the stairs as quietly as they could, the silence facilitated by the carpet. When they reached the front room, the door was closed. Strayhorn reached for it, but Loomis waved him away.

Strayhorn looked at Loomis with a questioning expression on his face.

Loomis cocked his pistol and aimed it at the door, then indicated that the others should do the same.

"Now!" he shouted.

All five men began blazing away at the door. Dust and sawdust flew out from the door as it filled with bullet holes. Shafts of sunlight stabbed through the holes. The noise of the gunshots bounced back from the walls of the hall so that, by the time they had expended their last round, their ears were ringing.

"Do you think we got 'em?" Luke asked, having to yell to be heard.

"Reload," Loomis ordered.

Quickly, the five men reloaded; then, with pistols at the ready, Loomis opened the door and they rushed into the room.

Inside the room, they saw evidence of the fusillade they had just unleashed. The window was shot out, the mirror was broken, there were holes in the dresser, in the walls, and in the bed.

But there were no MacCallisters.

"Where the hell did they go?" Seth asked.

Loomis stepped up to the window and looked out over the town. He was about to look away when he saw something that he hadn't seen before. There was something hanging from the signpost in the middle of town, the post that announced the intersection of Lincoln and Pine Streets.

"I'll be damned," he said.

"What? What is it?" Logan asked.

Loomis pointed. "The money," he said. "The son of a bitch has hung those saddlebags, with the money, from that signpost down there."

"Maybe he's saying this is the end of it," Logan said. "Maybe he's leavin' us the money, hopin' we'll go away."

"Maybe," Loomis said. "But I doubt it."

"I doubt it too. There's probably no money in 'em," Strayhorn said. "That's probably just the empty saddlebags."

"Nope," Loomis insisted, shaking his head. "I'm not sure what he is tryin' to do, but I believe the money is in them saddlebags."

"Why do you think that?"

"Because that's just the kind of thing that son of a bitch would do," Loomis said.

"So, what do we do now?" Luke asked.

"We go get the money," Loomis answered.

Falcon and Andrew were standing just under the overhang of the blacksmith shop, looking down the street toward the saddlebags.

"There are five of them," Falcon said. "I thought there were only three. Were those other two with them when they were holding you and Rosanna prisoner?"

"No," Andrew said. "This is the first I've seen of them."

"They must've signed on some help," Falcon said. He sighed. "Andrew, it's not too late for you to leave."

Andrew picked up a pair of blacksmith tongs. "If you say that again, little brother, I'm going to go right upside your head."

Falcon chuckled. "All right," he said. "It's your funeral."

"Ouch. You could have come up with a better cliché than that."

"I'm not worried, though," Falcon said.

"You aren't?"

"Nah. Here you are, standing right by my side, the same way you stood by Wyatt Earp's side in Tombstone," Falcon said.

Andrew laughed. "All right, I deserved that."

Loomis stuck his hand down into one of the saddlebags, then pulled out a fistful of money.

"Ha!" he shouted, holding the money over his head. "I told you! I told you the son of bitch would leave the money in the saddlebags!"

The others came running up to the signpost then, and there was a frenzy as they started pulling bound packets of money from the saddlebags and sticking them in their pockets.

"Remember, half of it is mine!" Loomis shouted.

"The hell it is!" Seth replied. "It's ever' man for himself now!"

The men started fighting among themselves, trying to grab the saddlebags from each other, dropping packets of money in their greedy attempt to get more.

"Well, now," Falcon suddenly said loudly.

"What do you think, Andrew? Isn't this like a bunch of flies, buzzing around a pile of horse turds?"

"You are insulting the flies, little brother," Andrew replied loudly.

"It's MacCallister!" Loomis shouted, grabbing for his gun.

Rosanna was in the dress shop across the way, watching through the window. She saw one of the men aiming at Andrew, holding his gun at arm's length. There was something unreal about it, as if she were watching Andrew performing a drama on stage. But it was Falcon who got his gun out first and the first shot came from his gun.

Despite the fact that one of the men was aiming at Andrew, Falcon fired at Loomis, who was the leader of the group. Rosanna saw the recoil kick Falcon's hand up, and she saw the great puff of smoke from the discharge. She heard Loomis call out in pain, then saw him grab his stomach as he went down.

After that, guns began to roar in rapid succession, and she saw that, though the first man seemed to have the drop on Andrew, his shot missed, whereas Andrew's shot did not. The man went down; then Andrew turned his attention toward Logan. Andrew and Logan fired at the same time, and Logan went down. As Logan was going down, she saw Falcon drop the second man that she didn't know, then turn his attention to Strayhorn. Strayhorn staggered back from being hit, then tried to raise his pistol to fire. This time both Falcon and Andrew fired, and Strayhorn was knocked flat on his back.

The entire battle was over within twenty seconds, and now Falcon and Andrew, the only two left on their feet, stood there looking down at the five bodies. Smoke curled up from the ends of their pistols to join with the larger cloud of gun smoke that was floating out over the town.

It was over.

From the far end of the street, the doors to the church opened and the townspeople, who had been convinced to take shelter, now started running up the street shouting in excitement and curiosity.

Andrew stood holding a smoking pistol, looking down at the men he had just bested.

"Oh, sir!" Rosanna said, holding her hand across her heart. "You have saved the town. You have bested the evil killer of men and despoiler of women."

"It was nothing," Andrew replied in a loud, clear voice.

"Nothing? Why, sir, you are too modest. What you did required courage and great skill."

"My adversary also had courage and skill," Andrew said. "But what made the difference in this contest was the triumph of good over evil."

"Yes," Rosanna said, her eyes shining brightly. "And thus it will always be — good over evil."

The curtains closed.

The curtains opened again, to the continuing applause of the audience. Andrew held out his hand to welcome the other players on stage, appearing in reverse order of their importance to the play.

The other players came out in ones and twos, until finally, all were standing on the stage. Then, taking each other's hand, Andrew and Rosanna stepped to the front for one final bow.

As they left the stage to go back to their dressing room, they were met by a reporter for the *New York Times*.

"Mr. MacCallister," the reporter said. "I have heard that this play is taken from real life. That it is a factual representation of your own exploits during your recent trip to the West. Is that true?"

Andrew looked over at Rosanna and smiled, then looked back at the reporter. He shook his head.

"It's just a play," he said. "A drama for the stage, and nothing more."

ABOUT THE AUTHORS

William W. Johnstone is the *USA Today* and *New York Times* bestselling author of over 220 books, including *The First Mountain Man, The Last Mountain Man, Blood Bond, Eagles, A Town Called Fury, Savage Texas, Matt Jensen, The Last Mountain Man: The Family Jensen, Sidewinders, The Last Gunfighter,* and the stand-alone thrillers *Vengeance is Mine, Invasion USA Border War, Remember the Alamo, Jackknife* and *Home Invasion.* Visit his website at www.william johnstone.net or by email at dogcia2006@ aol.com.

Being the all around assistant, typist, researcher, and fact checker to one of the most popular western authors of all time, **J. A. Johnstone** learned from the master, Uncle William W. Johnstone.

Bill, as he preferred to be called, began tutoring J.A. at an early age. After-school hours were often spent retyping manuscripts or researching his massive American Western History library as well as the more modern wars and conflicts. J.A. worked hard — and learned.

"Every day with Bill was an adventure story in itself, Bill taught me all he could about the art of storytelling and creating believable characters. *'Keep the historical facts accurate,'* he would say. *'Remember the readers, and as your grandfather once told me, I am telling you now: be the best J. A. Johnstone you can be.'*"